SKILLED IN MAGIC

FIVE ON AN ANCIENT TRAIL

GEMMA KIRKMAN

Copyright © 2019 Gemma Kirkman

ISBN: 978-1-925952-20-9
Published by Vivid Publishing
A division of Fontaine Publishing Group
P.O. Box 948, Fremantle
Western Australia 6959
www.vividpublishing.com.au

A catalogue record for this
book is available from the
National Library of Australia

1

Lee, Edward, Julian, Maggie and Enid stood in the main hall of the Professor's house, looking around them at the tapestries that adorned every wall. One in particular held their interest. It was highly unusual. To begin with, it appeared to be playing music.

"What's that sound?" Edward squinted at the large, detailed tapestry, trying to make sense of it. Low, melodic notes drifted out from between the threads, which formed the image of a dimly lit bar with a piano in the corner and a singer standing by it on a small stage, grasping a microphone.

The singer moved slightly, and appeared to look towards them.

Maggie squealed.

"Don't worry," Julian said, hugging his younger sister. "Lee . . . !" he called as she took a step closer. "Be careful!"

Lee was more curious than afraid. She moved even closer before turning around to face her brothers and sisters. "It seems fine . . ." she began.

With a sudden movement, the singer reached out and grabbed Lee's shoulder.

Enid and Maggie screamed as the boys rushed to rescue

Lee. Julian got to her first, pulling her back to stand with the group. Edward settled for pushing the singer's arm back into the tapestry with a tense shove. Lee stumbled slightly but soon regained her composure. Each of them looked curiously at the singer. She was beautiful and formidable, with a glorious mane of red curls that cascaded down her shoulders, falling to her hips. She wore a short, pretty red dress.

The microphone in the singer's hand was pointed at them like a weapon. She traced small circles in the air with it while appearing to yell at them, yet as she opened and closed her mouth, all was silent. The singer shook her head, looking frustrated that she could not be heard. She put one hand on her hip and pushed the microphone out of the tapestry so it protruded from the wall like a weird appendage.

"What do we do?" Enid asked, a slight tremor in her voice. Her blue eyes grew huge as she looked up at the shape-shifting tapestry.

"Here." Edward took a step forward and grabbed the microphone. With a swift motion, he jerked it out of the singer's hands. It fell to the floor with a clatter.

The others yelled at him.

"Edward!"

"What are you doing?!"

"Edward, don't!"

Enid didn't say anything. She just stared down at the microphone on the floor.

The singer smiled and mockingly blew them a kiss. She then backed away from the frame of the picture, promptly disappearing.

There were a few moments of silence.

"I think the tapestry's gone back to normal," Maggie said eventually.

They stared at it expectantly. It looked dense and flat again, like a normal wall hanging. Julian briefly ran his hand over it, then gave a terse nod to his siblings.

Edward tossed his messy blond hair. "You can't say you're not curious as well." He picked up the microphone and turned it over in his hands. Then, somewhat dramatically, he held it up like a sword.

Lee rolled her eyes and went to take it from him. A small tug-of-war later she was examining the microphone closely. It looked normal enough. It was black, with a slim, shiny handle and a rounded top. A thin line of crystal quartz ran around the joint between the handle and top, sparkling in the light.

Edward snatched it back from her. "Testing one, two, three!" His blue eyes shone with glee. He twirled it with a flourish and stared at it expectantly. Nothing happened. He shrugged. "Well, that was a bit of a washout." He spun the microphone again twice, then, after tapping it a few times, started to look annoyed.

"Give it to Enid," Lee said quickly, sensing her brother's usual impatience was close to erupting.

"Here," he said brusquely as he handed it to his little

sister. Enid put it carefully in her pocket, and Lee smiled at her obvious delight. Enid's feelings were more obvious to Lee than to people in general, because her magical gift was the ability to sense the intentions of the people around her.

"The Professor would have known what it meant," Maggie said, her voice catching. She closed her eyes briefly. Julian looked at her, frowning slightly. They were all still struggling to cope after the traumatic event in which they'd lost their guardian.

"What are we going to do now, without the Professor?" Maggie asked, her eyes glistening.

Julian put his arm around her shoulders and said heartily, "Don't worry, he taught us loads while he was here. We'll be okay." His arm tightened around Maggie's shoulders. "We've always been able to rely on each other."

It was true. The loss of their parents while they were all so young meant the Delliks had grown up to be very independent.

Maggie started to cry in earnest. She looked over at Julian, her violet eyes rimmed with red. "But what are we going to do now? Should we stay here, in the house? Or should we go?"

Julian had been contemplating the same thing. He nodded firmly, his mind made up. "Yes, we will. The Professor would have wanted us to stay here. He *did* build the house especially for us."

"Even for you, Enid," Lee said, smiling softly at her youngest sibling. Enid, only five years old, looked even smaller than her age. This was the first time she'd been in the house. Julian took this as an opportunity to distract Maggie.

"Maggie, why don't you show Enid around the house, and to her room?"

Maggie also looked younger than her ten years. Her fine features and the reddish-brown hair that bobbed on her shoulders made her look pixie-like.

"Okay," Maggie sniffled. She took Enid's hand and gave it a squeeze. "There are mice nearby that are talking to me." She gave a wobbly smile. She loved being able to talk to animals. It gave her a feeling of companionship when she was alone or upset.

Julian gave her a reassuring grin. "Well, show them to Enid then. I'm sure she'd love that!"

Maggie looked a little more cheerful. "They're the mouse babies I met before! They're all grown up now." Maggie smiled brightly while Enid's dimples flashed in excitement.

Julian smiled, but his grey eyes soon turned sombre as he watched the chattering girls leave the room. He understood how they felt all too well.

Despite their sorrow, they were also filled with happiness with the rescue of Enid. She'd been kidnapped as a baby by an evil magician, Mediarn, who had targeted their family because of their magical powers. They'd recently been reunited with her after many years of separation. But while they were thrilled at having her with them, they also felt dejected and a little lost without the Professor.

He'd been their guardian and a mentor to them, helping them to develop their powers and safeguard them on their quest to find Enid. It was a terrible loss now that he was no longer with them.

After dinner that night, Julian directed them all to head to bed and get a good night's sleep, which they did with barely a murmur.

* * *

The next morning at breakfast, Julian lowered his voice to speak to the older two of his siblings.

"Lee, Ed." Julian tilted his head conspiratorially. Edward perked up and raised his eyebrows. Lee played with her long brown hair and squinted at him with more reservation.

"What?" Lee and Edward said in unison, but in very different tones.

"Let's do something to cheer everyone up," Julian said, smiling.

Lee's bright green eyes shone. "That's a great idea!"

Edward was nodding rapidly as well. "Let's go for a horse ride, maybe?"

"And take a picnic!" Julian chipped in.

"I can make a cake!" Lee exclaimed. Her cakes were legendary.

"Great, we haven't had one of your cakes for ages!" Edward said, smacking his lips.

"Okay. Lee, you organise the food. Edward, get the

horses. And I'll go get us blankets, drinks and a basket." Julian counted each item on his fingers as he fired off orders.

"Yes sir!" Edward saluted with a cheeky grin, scampering off before Julian could respond.

Lee walked down one of the many corridors that branched off from the hallway. The house was complex in its design, and they'd discovered there was more to it than met the eye. Beyond the main room with the tapestries were four corridors branching off from it.

Maggie and Enid had headed down one of the corridors after breakfast, towards the bedrooms. Lee travelled down a corridor that led to three archways, and paused by one. She surveyed the study beyond it, with its wall-to-ceiling bookshelves and copper ladder that ran parallel to them on small wheels. Her eyes blurred as she remembered the Professor sitting behind the large wooden desk. Lee blinked rapidly and moved to the next archway, walking through it to the dining room and into the kitchen. She made a beeline to the nearest cupboard and opened it.

"Lee." Maggie appeared with Enid trailing close behind. "What are you doing?"

Lee poked her head out from behind the cupboard door. "Julian suggested we go on a horse ride and take a picnic."

Maggie's eyes brightened. "What a great idea! Yay, we have the place to ourselves!" she said with a grin. The usual kitchen staff had the day off. "We can make whatever we like." She smiled at Enid, who was glancing around the kitchen with an uncertain expression.

"I've got butter, sugar and vanilla. We need flour, eggs and a cake tin," Lee called.

"Check, check... and check," Maggie's voice was muffled as she dug into the bottom drawer for a tin. "Which one?" she asked, holding up two—one butterfly-shaped and the other heart-shaped.

"Butterfly!" Lee and Maggie chorused, and smiled at the memory of the magical ending to their last adventure.

"We need milk next," called Lee.

Enid opened the fridge and used both hands to take out the carton. "Check!"

Maggie and Lee giggled as Enid lumbered across the kitchen, half dragging the huge two-litre milk container along with her.

"Okay, I think that's everything," said Lee. She was perched at the counter with the mixing bowl, cake tin and ingredients in front of her.

"Why don't you help me mix the batter?" Lee said to Enid. She picked her little sister up and planted her on the bench next to the mixing bowl. "Aw, you're so eenie and small!" Lee looked at her fondly.

Enid's dimples flashed in reply.

"Eenie! What a great nickname for you!" Maggie chuckled.

Lee laughed. "It's perfect!" And so, the nickname stuck.

Lee got to work with the mixture, pouring in various ingredients. She pushed the cord of the electric egg-beater into the power plug and switched it on. With a *whirrrrr* it started up. Lee whipped the ingredients into a lather.

Intrigued, Eenie bent closer to the bowl to look, her long blond hair dangling over her face.

"AAAAAAAAARGGHHHHHHHH!"

"EENIE!"

The beaters made a sad choking sound as they whirred to a stop. Eenie's hair had become caught in them and churned into the mixture.

Eenie gave a strangled cry and sat up in shock. The beaters clung to the side of head, her hair twisted up in the metal whisks.

"Oh, EENIE!" Lee exclaimed in horror.

Maggie started laughing weakly at their expressions.

"Maggie, that isn't helping." Lee pulled Eenie to her and surveyed the damage. It was a total mess. Her blond hair was tangled in a huge knot with the two metal whisks sticking out the side. Lee pulled the cord out of the wall as Eenie stared at her with huge blue eyes. Her mouth quivered.

Lee waited for her to burst into tears.

Eenie opened her mouth . . . and a peal of laughter rang out. Lee blinked. Maggie gulped back the giggles, shoulders shaking as she tried, unsuccessfully, to sponge off the mixture. Lee shook her head in bemusement, looking around at the mess. Cake mixture had been flung across the countertop and onto the floor, and all three of the girls had been sprayed with droplets of gooey batter.

Eenie laughed peal after peal, her small shoulders shaking. Maggie half-heartedly attempted to extract hair from the beaters, or perhaps the other way around, and snorted at Eenie's high-pitched giggles. Maggie and Eenie soon had tears streaming down their cheeks. One would slowly stop laughing, then catch the other's eye, and they were off again.

The boys walked in, having heard the commotion. Shock at the state of the kitchen changed to sniggers as they took in the scene. All three girls were in stitches, with poor little Eenie still sitting on the kitchen counter with the whisks stuck in her hair.

Chaos ensued as everyone had a go pulling Eenie's hair free of the whisks. Julian was eventually successful after carefully twisting her hair and washing it under the tap at the same time.

"Well, so much for a cake!" Lee shrugged as she surveyed the mess in the kitchen. "There's no time to make one now, we'll just have to do without."

"Come on, let's get going," Edward said, tapping his wristwatch. "I have five horses in the stables, saddled up. Grab whatever you can from the kitchen, and let's go!"

The others needed little encouragement, and soon all five were ready to go, chattering excitedly and looking forward to the ride.

2

The five children walked across the meadow towards the stables, hand in hand. "My palms still twinge when we hold hands," said Maggie, letting go of Julian's and Lee's and shaking her own slightly. She was referring to the birthmarks on each of their palms—five small dots that showed up as faint white patches of skin.

"Why wouldn't they?" Lee asked, rubbing her palm.

Maggie shrugged. "I thought maybe the five-as-one power was a one-time thing." She was referring to a unique ability they had recently discovered when they rescued Enid. When the four of them stood in a circle with Enid in the middle, she seemed to become a channel for something powerful and magnificent. It had ended up being the evil magician, Mediarn's, downfall.

"Our powers aren't a once-off though," said Edward, picking up a nearby stone and turning it into a bright red ball. His magic power was that he could change any object at will. He threw it up into the air with a flourish, then caught it and aimed it at the back of Lee's head.

She knew him too well and had already turned to catch the ball before it left his hand. *Edward's power can be as obnoxious as he is*, thought Lee with a scowl.

"There's no reason why the five-as-one power wouldn't still work," said Julian as he picked up Eenie and swung her up onto his shoulders. The little girl shrieked in excitement.

"I'm curious about it though," said Lee. "We should practise it again." She taunted Edward with the red ball, tossing it from hand to hand.

Julian frowned. "I don't think that's a good idea. We don't know how to control the power, and last time we used it to defeat something evil, so who knows what would happen if we used it again now."

Lee threw the ball as hard as she could at Julian. "Wimp!" she cried, laughing as her brother, eyebrows raised, easily caught it. His power was he could move anything with his mind. The ball left his hand and shot upwards, where it hovered mid-air above them all. Julian's power was easily the most potent of them all.

Lee looked at at her siblings and thought about how different each of their powers were. Her own power to sense people's intentions, and occasionally to see into the future, sometimes made her feel hesitant and uncertain, because she could never truly be sure of what might happen when she used it. It was also frustrating to not be able to call upon her power at will, like her siblings could.

"Come on, Lee, you're falling behind!" Maggie called. She was right; Lee was trailing behind, lost in her thoughts.

"Coming!" Lee sprinted and quickly caught up with the others as they arrived at the stables. As they drew closer, they heard the whinnying and stamping of the horses.

"It smells funny," Eenie said, wrinkling up her nose.

"It's the manure, and that sweaty horse smell," said Maggie.

"Yuck!" Eenie wrinkled up her nose up even more.

Maggie smiled and shrugged. "I actually like it." Her eyes looked a little unfocused for a minute as she talked to the horses. "I want to ride the chestnut one. He's lovely."

Maggie's ability to communicate telepathically with animals often made her appear introverted and shy. Lee often thought her sister seemed detached from the world outside her head. Lee also suspected Maggie would have been just as shy if she didn't talk to animals.

"I've got the white one!" cried Edward as he led them around the corner to where the five waiting horses were already saddled. The white horse was a magnificent stallion, the biggest of the five. He stamped his hooves when he saw the group.

Julian made a beeline for the small, spotted pony and helped Eenie up onto it. Maggie and Edward were already on their horses, who stamped with impatience as the others mounted. Lee looked at the dark bay draft horse with a smile. She couldn't sense the intentions of animals, but he appeared calm and placid as she swung herself up onto his broad back. Julian sat astride the dappled-grey mare shortly after, and the horses started moving restlessly in anticipation.

Maggie gave a nod, and they were off.

* * *

Cantering over the rolling green meadows, wind in their hair, the siblings shouted to each other, affectionately trading insults back and forth.

As hooves pounded grass, Edward and Lee urged their horses on, trying to race each other.

"You'll never beat me!" Edward yelled in challenge. Lee pursed her lips and dug in her heels. They quickly approached the forest in the distance. Julian's call for them to slow down was lost to the wind.

Lee leant forward over her horse, determined to win. She and Edward were soon miles ahead of the others, with Lee leading by a few seconds. Her temples ached in a familiar way that told her she was about to have a vision. Though she'd learnt how to deal with these visions so they weren't overwhelming, it was still hard for her to accept the sudden and distracting impact they made. *No one understands how difficult it can be*, she thought, rubbing her temples with one free hand.

Edward yelled something indistinguishable.

She raised her fist in challenge and leant onto the horse's neck to make him go faster.

"Catch me if you can!" Lee yelled in return, with a sudden, furious urge to win.

Edward yelled something back that was snatched by the wind. He gave his horse a sharp slap on the rear.

Lee focused her will to win. "Come on, come on, come

on!" She felt another sudden surge in her temples, much stronger than the last. Ignoring the feeling, she dug in her heels and gritted her teeth. The next surge came. It was overwhelming, and she blacked out.

* * *

A lady stood before her.

She was wearing a long white dress that rippled over her pale skin in the breeze.

Her white hair was twisted up into many curly knots of different sizes, from which small tufts stuck out here and there.

Her pale eyes had a clear sheen to them, and her pupils were dilated.

She opened her mouth to speak . . .

* * *

"Lee! Lee! Are you okay?"

Lee awoke to find Edward shaking her shoulder. She groaned and felt the damp, soggy grass beneath her. She pushed Edward's hand from her shoulder and sat up.

"I'm fine, I'm fine!" Lee brushed the grass away. "I just fell off, that's all."

The others had caught up and looked concerned. Lee brushed aside their questions. She stood up and swung herself back into the saddle.

"I'm fine, really! My horse stumbled, and I lost my

balance." Lee caught Edward hiding a smirk. She felt cross and decided not to tell them about her vision. "Come on, let's get going."

She smartly turned her horse around and gestured for the others to do the same. As she did so, Lee looked over her shoulder and saw a pale arm slink behind an oak tree. Blinking, she looked again, but there was nothing, only the dark bark of the old tree.

It must be an after effect of the vision, Lee thought, and dismissed it.

They spent the next couple of hours cantering across green fields, stopping only to enjoy their picnic. The few hours in the sun and wind left the group with red rosy cheeks and huge grins.

As the sun started to sink on the horizon, they headed home, laughing and chattering. Approaching the stables, they noticed a familiar figure standing on the fringes of the field.

"Mr Lennon!" they cried in unison.

It was their friend they had met during the course of their many adventures; he'd helped them out enormously when they'd rescued Enid.

"How did you get here!" Maggie exclaimed.

Mr Lennon gave a short laugh. "I knew the Professor well, remember? I know about the blue-moon door, the one that allows people to cross over from other worlds into this house."

Edward looked at him with astonishment. "We used it

to cross into the blue world. What do you mean, it allows people to cross over from other worlds?"

Mr Lennon gave another short laugh. "There's much you don't know, young one."

Edward looked a little insulted.

"Young?" he muttered under his breath, annoyed. "I'm *twelve!*"

"Boys are far more immature than girls," Lee said smugly.

Edward snorted.

"'The blue world', you say," Mr Lennon queried with a twist to his mouth.

"That's what it was," Edward said defensively.

Mr Lennon looked down his nose. "It has a far more noble name than that!" he said with derision. "That world is called Partior."

"I prefer 'the blue world'," Edward said in an undertone. Lee smirked despite herself and nudged him to be quiet.

"The other dark worlds you went through are known as Aequalis . . ."

"The one where everything floated," Julian said in a low undertone.

". . . and Consecutio," Mr Lennon finished.

"The jungle where . . ." Edward looked at Lee quickly.

"What was Mediarn's world called?" Maggie asked curiously.

"Libertas," Mr Lennon said shortly, glancing sideways at Edward. Lee remembered the tall, imposing glass and steel buildings, the magic shop, and the frantic bustling crowd.

She surveyed Mr Lennon, eyes narrowed. He had always intrigued her. For one, he was enormously tall, towering over the group as he spoke to them. He seemed to be growing a beard as his whiskers were considerably longer than last time; tinged with red, and covering half his face. He looked very serious as he addressed the group. "I have to tell you all something."

They waited expectantly.

Mr Lennon cleared his throat. "I think the Professor may still be alive."

Loud shrieks and gasps met his words.

"What do you mean, he's still alive?" Julian half shouted. He lowered his voice as Mr Lennon flinched. "Sorry", he said. "I can't believe it. What do you mean, *alive*?"

"Alive! Really?" Maggie and Lee held no such reservations, and clutched one another in excitement. Eenie stood off to the side watching them, her hands held together in front of her.

"Alive?" Edward snorted, sounding more doubtful than excited.

Julian's face was white as he stared at Mr Lennon, awaiting a response.

Mr Lennon put his hand up and said in a commanding voice, "He could be. It's not certain!" He gestured for the group to sit under a nearby tree as he continued the story. They sat cross-legged and looked up at him with bright eyes. Lee felt Edward's intention to say something sarcastic, and she put her hand on his arm as a warning. He shrugged her off and waited for Mr Lennon to continue.

"Have you heard the music?" Mr Lennon asked.

The five children looked at him, bemused.

"From the musicians," he explained.

The group looked at each other, then back at Mr Lennon expectantly.

"What music?" they asked, exclaimed in unison.

Mr Lennon shook his head impatiently. "Never mind. There is music being played by musicians in the dark worlds." He paused, looking a little surprised. "And your world." He went on. "You know that music contains hidden messages, don't you?"

The group stared at him, unsure of how to reply. Edward was the first to pipe up. "Do the lyrics in the music talk about the Professor?"

"Lyrics?" Mr Lennon looked at Edward intently. "No," he said, frowning. "It's true that words have power, especially when combined with music. But it is within the vibration and frequency that the messages lie."

Edward pulled a face but listened carefully as Mr Lennon continued. "The music is saying something right now." He cupped his ear, as if he could hear it in the wind. "It has a strange vibration within it." Mr Lennon crouched down so he was eye level with the five. "I'm almost sure it's about the Professor. You remember his power?"

"He could disappear and reappear at will," said Maggie, blinking at him.

"Precisely," said Mr Lennon. "I think the music refers to that power."

"But we saw his body," Edward retorted.

Julian looked down. Lee moved slightly so she was sitting closer to him.

"There are forces in this world the Professor was friendly with," Mr Lennon explained. "I believe someone, or something, carried his body away."

The siblings shifted uneasily and looked at one another. They pondered this for a moment.

Mr Lennon continued. "I believe he rests in a deep slumber, but the five-as-one power may be strong enough to awaken him." He looked at the group with something akin to respect. "You will need to find the Professor. Even I don't know where he is. But he would have left clues behind at every stage of his travels, so someone could find him if he ever needed to be found."

"What travels?" asked Maggie.

"He travelled far and wide before he built this house," Mr Lennon explained.

"The Professor did mention that, actually," said Lee. She thought back to when she had questioned the Professor about his travels, not too long after they had first met him. The memory made her smile. *He also mentioned he'd built the house around the blue-moon doorway*, she thought absently.

"So, we just go through the blue-moon door and start there again?" Julian said, a small crease appearing between his brows.

Mr Lennon grimaced. "Don't be foolish. Of course not."

"How are we going to retrace the Professor's travels,

then?" Julian asked, the crease deepening.

Mr Lennon glanced at him. "It's true the Professor travelled through the other worlds," he said, his voice softening a little. "But . . ." He paused. "He mostly travelled through *your* world."

"*Our* world?" Lee exclaimed.

"Yes. You have many continents, yes?" Mr Lennon gave a curt nod. "He will most likely be on one of them." He stood up. "You must find him using the clues he left behind."

"What kind of clues?" Edward asked.

Mr Lennon shrugged. "I'm afraid I don't know."

"Where do we start, then?" Julian asked.

"I don't know."

"Where did he travel to?" Lee asked.

"I don't know."

"Do you know anything?" This sarcasm came from Edward.

Mr Lennon raised an eyebrow.

Lee shot Edward a look. It was no good asking more questions, because they soon realised they were going round in circles. It was clear Mr Lennon knew nothing about the Professor's whereabouts.

Brushing the grass off, the five stood up. Lee invited Mr Lennon to come back to the house.

"No, thank you, I must be off," he said.

"What's *your* power, Mr Lennon?" Maggie suddenly asked.

He gave her a rare smile. "I'm fortunate enough to be able to play any instrument I turn my hand to."

Maggie and Lee sucked in their breath quickly, impressed.

Eenie stood behind Julian's leg and peeped out at the imposing figure from behind him.

"I'd love to be able to do that," Edward said enviously.

Mr Lennon paused and surveyed them. "There's one thing that might help you."

They looked back at him, interested.

"I *do* know . . ." he said, pausing deliberately and with a level look at Edward, "that you've started working out the secrets of the tapestries."

"What secrets?" Maggie asked.

"I believe you have an instrument of music with you, little girl." Mr Lennon's lips twitched as he looked down at Julian's leg, to Eenie hiding behind him. The others softly cajoled her, and she came out of her hiding spot. Eenie slowly withdrew the microphone from her pocket. The tiny pieces of crystal caught the sunlight.

"That is no ordinary microphone," said Mr Lennon.

Edward grunted. "Pulling it out of a picture probably gave that away," he muttered to Lee. She nudged him, trying to listen.

"What I can tell you is, the microphone will amplify sounds," Mr Lennon explained.

"No kidding?" Edward said under his breath.

The Delliks watched him expectantly, but the statement

signalled the end of the conversation. Mr Lennon stood up and was evidently about to leave them. Lee cut Edward off before he could speak.

"Won't you stay longer?" Lee asked.

"I have to go, unfortunately," Mr Lennon said as he started to walk away.

"Wait! Sir!" Julian cried after him. "What if we need help?" He looked troubled.

Julian is always worried for us, Lee thought sympathetically.

Mr Lennon looked back at them. "Help is always there for those who ask for it," he said with a smile that disappeared as quickly as it came. "Now, I really must be off."

With a few more strides, he reached a stand of trees, and was gone.

3

The five were quiet that night as they sat at the dining table, each lost in their thoughts. Dinner was a subdued event. The waiting staff seemed to pick up on their mood and served the food in silence.

Despite the solemnity, the food was as delicious as always, and the atmosphere didn't stop their appetites. They tucked into large, juicy steaks served with a creamy diane sauce. Big, fluffy pieces of white bread were there to mop up the leftover sauce at the end.

Lee picked up Julian's mood more intensely than the others, and tried to draw him into conversation.

"What's wrong?" she asked in a low voice.

He shot a quick glance at the others. Seeing they were distracted with their meals, he replied in a quiet voice, "I just feel so guilty about the Professor."

"What?" Lee exclaimed. "Why should you feel guilty?"

"I couldn't stop the sword, could I?" he said, his grey eyes darker than usual.

"Oh, Julian." Lee was silent, trying to find the words to comfort her brother. "You did everything you could have," she said finally, squeezing his forearm. He gave her a small smile, but moved his arm away gently to reach for another helping of food.

The moment passed, and Lee picked up her fork, joining in with the muted conversation that had sprung up between her siblings.

* * *

The morning light hit Lee with a blinding glare.

"Come on, slowpoke, breakfast is already on the table!" Maggie called in to her.

Lee pulled the pillow over her head and tried to get a few more minutes of sleep. Eenie came in giggling, and with Maggie's encouragement climbed into the bed with Lee.

"Eeeeenie!" Lee groaned. She didn't have the heart to chastise her little sister, as Maggie well knew, so she gave in and got up.

The boys were already at the kitchen table when the girls trooped in.

"What's for breakfast?" Lee asked, her hunger suddenly kicking in. Sitting before them on the table were soft-boiled eggs and thick, buttery toast cut into long soldiers.

"That's your third egg, Edward," Julian said as his brother dunked a toast soldier into an eggcup, causing bright yellow yolk to overflow.

"So what?" he said between bites. "I'm a growing lad!"

Lee snorted. "More like a growing pig."

Edward threw a bit of toast at her. Julian used his powers to stall it mid-air. It then fell to the table. With a laugh

Edward changed the toast into a black beetle, causing the girls to scream and scoot back their chairs.

"Edward!" Julian said sternly.

Edward shrugged and changed the beetle back into toast. Maggie grimaced and threw the toast in the bin.

"So, how do we retrace the Professor's travels?" Lee asked, cautiously helping herself to a toast soldier from the rack. The question had the desired effect, and they all shrugged, albeit somewhat glumly.

"Who knows?" Julian sighed.

"How can we possibly know where to start looking?" Maggie asked.

"Maybe we can start in his study." Edward mused.

Eenie looked around at the others. "I saw the Professor!" she said. All eyes turned to her. She blinked hard and looked at the floor.

"What do you mean, you saw the Professor?" said Maggie, smiling indulgently.

"I saw him in the tapestry in the hall," said Eenie in a small voice.

The others looked at each other, open-mouthed.

"Of course! He's in the tapestry!" Maggie said, her voice shrill. Together they leapt from their seats and ran out of the kitchen, breakfasts forgotten.

They skidded to a halt in the main hall, looking around at the dozens of tapestries, each of them unique. Maggie made a beeline for one of them, the one they now knew well, with the five strangely drawn figures that represented themselves—the Delliks children, and the five-as-one power. The others followed, and soon all five were enthralled by what they saw in the brightly coloured tapestry amongst the black, white and shades of orange.

Where there were once only five figures, a sixth had appeared at the end of their last adventures, clumsily drawn like the others, standing to one side, observing the scene.

Edward squinted. "It's hard to see, but it's definitely . . ."

"Professor!" Maggie cried with a catch in her voice. "Professor?" she called, peering at the figure intently.

Lee ran her hand over the tapestry, but it was smooth and unmoving. "It's not like the other tapestry."

"At least we got a microphone out of that one," said Edward with a tiny smirk.

The words triggered something in Lee. "The microphone! Try the microphone!"

Maggie winced. "Don't yell so loud."

"Sorry!" Lee said, too excited to lower her voice. "Surely that's it!"

"Eenie, get it out," Edward said.

Eenie fumbled with the microphone. With a quivering hand, she raised it up to the sixth figure.

There was an expectant pause.

"Do you . . ." Maggie began.

"SHHHHHH!"

Silence again.

Then softly, almost too faint to hear, a low crackling noise emitted from the microphone.

Maggie and Lee gasped. Edward furiously waved at them to be quiet. He pushed Eenie's hand to hold the microphone closer. She was almost too short to reach so stood on her tippy-toes.

The low crackling cleared slightly until a faint whisper could be heard.

"*Roam . . . Roam . . . Roam . . .*" It was faint, but it was clearly the Professor's voice. "*Roam . . .*"

The five whooped and grabbed each other.

"It worked!" Lee gave Eenie a quick hug. Maggie and Julian put their arms around each other in delight.

"Do it again!" said Edward, and Eenie held the microphone to the tapestry once more.

"*Roam . . . Roam . . . Roam . . .*"

The word repeated a few more times before fading into silence.

"Roam!" Julian exclaimed. "Roam where?"

"I think that's the only word," Maggie said.

Eenie held the microphone up a few moments longer until her little arm started quivering at the effort. Lee's powers were useful at times like this, and sensing Eenie growing anxious with the effort and attention said, "Thanks Eenie, you did great." Lee gently lowered her little sister's arm. Eenie looked relieved and put the microphone carefully back in her pocket.

Lee looked around at the others, noticing their mixed reactions. Maggie looked happy and kept gazing at the tapestry and the Professor's figure.

Julian looked a little anxious. "Roam where?" he said again.

Edward stared at the tapestry with one eyebrow raised.

"Mr Lennon said we had to retrace his travels," Maggie said.

Edward frowned, looking thoughtful. He gave a sudden shout making them all jump. "Not 'roam' . . . 'Rome'!" The others looked at him blankly. "As in Italy," he said impatiently.

Their expressions cleared, and they looked at each other excitedly.

"Of course! The Professor must have travelled to Rome!" Lee brought her hands together and rubbed them, grinning.

"How on earth are we supposed to get to Rome?" Julian said, the small crease of worry reappearing between his eyes. He looked a lot less excited than the others. "We need an adult to go on a plane. Plus, it'll take us ages to get there."

Lee rubbed her chin. "Could you lift something with all of us in it?"

"Maybe," Julian said. He blinked a couple of times, the crease between his eyes disappearing. "I've never tried it, but there's no reason why not."

Eenie looked excited. "Oooo, really!"

"What could we go in?" Maggie looked as excited as her little sister.

Edward gave a short laugh. "How about the bathtub?"

Julian started to chuckle and then stopped. He raised his eyebrows at his brother. "Actually, that's not a bad idea."

"I was kidding!"

"Well, it's something we might all squeeze into!" said Julian. Edward stared at him for a split second, then gave a wild grin and ran up the entranceway to the corridors. The others followed him, with a little less noise, down the corridors to the bathroom.

The five crowded into the small room and looked down at the bathtub. An old freestanding tub with strong claw-like feet, it was very large and made of shiny, white porcelain.

"It might work," said Julian as he surveyed it with half-lidded eyes. The bath made a small rocking motion as he tested his powers on it.

"Hang on . . ." Edward gripped the edges. The bathtub expanded until it was large enough to take them all. Julian grinned at his brother when he noticed the comfy cushioned bottom and sides.

The girls hopped into the bath at Julian's nod. Fits of giggles started up as they crowded each other in a tangle of gangly legs and elbows. It was a bit of a squeeze when the boys joined them, but Edward adjusted the roominess a couple more times until they were all comfortable.

Julian sat at the end and held the sides of the tub. He closed his eyes, forehead wrinkling as he concentrated.

The bathtub jerked slightly. Maggie and Eenie shrieked as the bathtub started to wiggle. Julian was completely still as the big porcelain bathtub began to slowly rise from the ground.

"Wait, Julian, do you still have the book?" Lee exclaimed suddenly. "We should probably take it with us!" The mystical relic they had discovered on their last adventures could come in handy. It had once belonged to their parents and only they could open it. It had helped them before, but it was erratic and often hard to interpret. *Still,* thought Lee, *it has magic between its pages. It might help us out again one day.*

"Good idea!" Julian said. "It's in my room." The bathtub had been hovering a couple of inches off the ground. It suddenly dropped to the floor with a thud, startling its occupants as it did so.

"I'll get it," Lee volunteered, clambering out of the bathtub.

"Shouldn't we take food and clothes with us as well?" Maggie, ever practical, suggested.

Edward shrugged. "I can make us what we need."

"The book's in my backpack," Julian called out as Lee ran towards their bedrooms.

* * *

Lee faced five doors brightly painted in different colours. She opened the blue door that led into Julian's bedroom. The backpack was lying on his bed, and she could see the corner of the book sticking out.

Lee pulled it out and surveyed it. It was somewhat tattered since their last adventure, and the strange swirl on the front cover was a bit tarnished.

Rubbing the book with her sleeve in a half-hearted attempt to clean it, Lee's palm made contact with the swirl. It began to move. Twisting and turning like a coiled snake, five beams of light slowly started to appear. The beams rose from the surface to make direct contact with the birthmark on her palm.

"Oops," Lee muttered guiltily. She hadn't meant to open it on her own.

The book ruffled its pages in a friendly manner. It was like the book was waving to her. Lee gave a small laugh. The book turned to the first page, entitled 'Skilled in Magic'. It gave a cheerful flick of the page, then turned over again.

Lee bent over to read the words.

To our darling Lee.
If you are reading this, the book has deemed you ready
to read our words to you.

Lee sat back up with a jerk, her heart racing. She looked back at the page and saw the signature 'Amelia and Mike Delliks' at its bottom. The words were from her parents!

"LEE, COME ON!" came the voices from further down the corridor.

There was no time. Lee slammed the book shut, raced out into the corridor, and back down to the bathroom.

Climbing into the bathtub, waving the book, she said with elation, "I've got it! Let's go!"

"We're off to Rome!" Edward said, throwing his hands

in the air suddenly, startling everyone. He clapped a sharp little ditty. Eenie giggled at him, and he grinned back at her, pulling her closer to him in a quick hug.

Maggie's face was alight with anticipation. "Rome! I can't wait!" she exclaimed. "I've always wanted to go there." She wriggled around in the bathtub, unable to sit still. "We learnt about it at school, and it looked so beautiful in the pictures."

"We might be able to spend my birthday there!" Lee said, her eyes turning a deep green as she thought back to school lessons. Beautiful architecture, cobbled alleyways and centuries-old monuments. She bumped shoulders with Maggie as they grinned widely at each other.

Eenie looked shyly from one of her sibling to another as they excitedly chatted between them. She looked tiny in her big jacket, which she had pulled around her, and which enveloped her further in its voluminous fabric.

The bathtub gave a lurch and all conversation stopped as they hung on tightly to the sides. It wobbled dangerously at one point, but as Julian gripped the sides and narrowed his eyes, it straightened up again.

It was a lot smoother once they were floating mid-air. Julian soon got the hang of keeping them straight. He did a few practice moves as they floated around the bathroom, and at their insistent urging to "HURRY UP!" and "LET'S GOOO!" sailed the bath merrily out of the door.

It felt very odd at first, flying through the corridors in a giant bathtub. Julian opened the front door and closed it behind him as they flew through. Lee could only wonder at his strength and discipline to make two things happen at once. She was impressed with her older brother, mentally comparing his progress to when they had first arrived at the house.

Flying smoothly outside, they rose higher and higher in the air until the trees below were tiny specks. The wind hit their faces surprisingly hard, and their cheeks and lips soon became bright pink from the force of it.

"Look!" Maggie pointed to a flock of birds in the distance. "They want to fly with us!" Maggie sat back happily as the flock of birds grew closer and formed a flying V around the bathtub. They were so close, any one of them could have put a hand out to touch them. Lee watched their feathers ruffle against the breeze as they flew straight as arrows next to their bathtub.

"Oooo, they're pretty!" Eenie looked delighted and sat up straighter to get a better look at their companions. Being the smallest of the group, she could barely see over the sides. Her little hands grasped the bathtub rim as she stared unblinkingly at the feathered creatures.

"They're ibises, Eenie," said Maggie, shifting slightly so she was closer to her little sister. She grasped the rim next to her and pointed out which one was the leader, which one had a sore wing from flying too long, and which one was the troublemaker of the group. The ibises flew up one by one as Maggie pointed them out, turning to stare at Eenie with their kind black eyes while clicking their curved, elongated black beaks. Eenie giggled. Happiness radiated off her like a warm glow.

"They're funny looking," Edward observed, pointing at the birds' long, spindly legs folded up underneath their bodies like bundles of twigs. "Aren't they the scavengers that eat junk from rubbish bins?"

"They're beautiful!" Maggie said hotly. "They're actually really intelligent and can fly thousands of miles." Her eyes were half closed as she spoke to them in her mind. "Julian, they know how to get to Rome!" She sat back, pleased. "They'll help us navigate."

"How do they know it's Rome?" Lee asked curiously. "They don't call it the same word as us, surely?"

Maggie giggled. "Of course not. I just projected them an image of where we want to go, and they recognised it from that."

"Well, that's handy," Edward said grudgingly. "Julian's sense of direction isn't even good when we're walking."

Julian was concentrating too hard to react much, but he managed to aim a kick at Edward's leg. Eenie climbed into Julian's lap and he hugged her to him.

"How long, Maggie?" Edward asked, rubbing his leg with a grimace.

"Won't be too long if you'd let Julian concentrate!" Maggie exclaimed, before looking back to admire the ibises as they streaked their way together through the sky.

4

They flew swiftly through the air. The birds glided effortlessly in front of them as the bathtub sliced through the air with only an occasional small wobble. The five crouched further down in the tub as the wind rushed furiously past them, messing up their hair and whistling in their ears. The clouds surrounding them looked like the softest of pillows. Lee put her hand out to try and touch one, but the cloud trickled through her fingers like steam from a kettle.

Maggie soon gave a shriek. "The birds say we're here!"

Edward looked at Julian with a raised eyebrow. Julian shrugged at the unasked question. "I don't know how we got here so quickly. It almost felt like some sort of bubble or cocoon was around us the whole way. I have no idea what it was."

"The wind wasn't as strong as I was expecting," Lee agreed.

The strangeness of the journey was forgotten as the group peered over the edge of the tub. They gasped in awe. Below them was a colossal, crumbling arena. Its huge walls encompassed rows and rows of limestone windows. It was free-standing, and a lot of the walls had caved in, but the view from above was magnificent. It was almost too daunting and complex for them to take in, and the five marvelled at lines upon lines of cavities and spaces surrounded by boulders and archways.

"It looks like an open-air theatre!" Maggie exclaimed.

"It IS an open-air theatre!" Lee cried.

"No it's not, it was used for fights," said Edward. "I think mostly with animals. Or between people and animals."

Maggie looked upset at this revelation, so Julian swiftly changed the subject. "I'll land us soon," he said. "Keep an eye out for a deserted patch where we won't be seen."

They were soon descending carefully though the sky, Julian painstakingly avoiding the people milling below, aiming for a patch of grass that the birds had scouted out for them. They descended a lot quicker than they expected as Julian didn't want anyone accidentally looking up into the sky and seeing a flying bathtub.

The wind blasted them as they fell out of the sky, the Delliks muffling small shrieks as they landed with a soft thud.

Edward shook his head, attempting to pop his blocked ears. "Not so fast next time!"

Piling out of the bathtub, the group stood and looked around. The day was fresh and bright. Vivid blue skies sat atop sprawling ancient architecture. Nearby was a particularly imposing structure, rising from the green grounds, magnificent and proud.

Standing together in the sunlight they looked up at the

structure in awe. "Wow, it's huge!" Edward exclaimed.

"It's the smallest country in the world," said Lee, reciting something she'd learnt at school.

"It's so pretty," Eenie said in a quiet and admiring tone.

"Let's go take a look," said Maggie, making a beeline for it. The others followed, trailing behind. They approached the huge space with its large paved floor encircled by daunting white pillars that spanned around it like a huge gate.

"I feel about two inches tall," Julian remarked as he turned in a semi-circle to take in more of the view.

"Imagine how Eenie feels then," said Edward, pulling lightly on his little sister's long blond braid. The others laughed at her grumpy expression as she pulled her head away.

Lee gazed up at the columns. Each had a statue perched atop. Scanning them with interest, she noticed how different each one was. Fashioned from marble, like the pillars, some statues were of scholars, holding books and posing dramatically; others were of stern-looking soldiers with swords, frozen in place and staring down at her.

Something moved suddenly out of the corner of her eye. Lee blinked and jerked her head around to stare at one of the statues. It was a woman in a flowing white dress. Lee could have sworn the statue's dress rippled slightly in the breeze. Staring harder at it, Lee took a quick intake of breath. She turned to tell Julian she recognised the statue, when a massive cheer went up from the crowd.

"Oh, look, there's a man coming out!" Maggie said,

pointing behind them. They turned to follow her outstretched finger.

A multitude of windows faced them above one of the walls of pillars. A fancy red flag rolled out from the window, and hung there like a banner. It was a deep velvet red, trimmed with gold. A small man wearing a white cap appeared at the window, and the crowd went wild at his appearance. The clapping and cheering of the crowd was deafening, and the Delliks clapped their hands to their ears at the din.

Lee suddenly lost all concentration as the crowd's emotions hit her like a tidal wave. She put out her hand weakly and clutched at Julian's arm to hold herself upright.

"Are you okay?" Julian asked, concerned.

She nodded vaguely.

"Come on, let's go. This crowd is too much for Lee," Julian said hastily, gesturing for them to move to the outskirts. They were used to Lee's reactions to large groups of people and rallied together by swiftly shepherding her out of the way of the surging crowd. Edward picked up Eenie into a piggy back as the crowd started to edge closer.

The small man with the white cap opened a large sheet of paper before him. He started reading from it in a powerful voice, throbbing with emotion. The crowd grew even rowdier as his voice resonated over the masses.

"I wonder what he's reading to them?" called Maggie over her shoulder. "I can't understand him." Julian had taken the lead, Lee leaning weakly on him as they pushed their way through the masses.

"He's speaking in Italian," Edward called back in a knowing tone.

The short man soon switched from Italian to French as the five got to the outskirts of the crowd. He switched languages one final time as his voice grew to a crescendo that indicated the speech was finishing.

"And now Spanish!" Edward said admiringly, as they finally left the crowd behind.

* * *

After a few minutes sitting on her own, her siblings chatting amongst themselves, Lee finally declared herself ready to walk properly again.

"Rome. An entire city. Couldn't be a broader clue if he tried," Edward grumbled, but good-naturedly.

All their spirits were considerably higher since they'd heard the Professor's voice. *Even so, Julian seemed more downcast than usual,* Lee thought. She made up her mind to check in on him later.

After chatting about the direction they should go, and making absolutely no headway, they started walking across the grounds in silent agreement, to at least feel they were doing something. Their aimless wandering eventually found them staring up at what appeared to be a gigantic stone wall.

"Looks a bit scary," Maggie commented as they blinked against the glimmering sun. The imposing border stretched around a curved 90-degree angle, and the daunting walls reached towards the sky for what seemed like miles.

"It's like a huge cement barricade," said Edward. The others murmured agreement. Julian pointed at a white archway. Atop were two stone figures, resting against a shield.

"That looks like an entrance," he said. "Let's go in and take a look."

As the group drew closer, they realised in dismay that the queue to get in was massive and snaked halfway around the block. They obediently joined the line at the end. After a few moments it became apparent people were staring at them. The looks from the people around them were mostly aimed at Eenie and Edward, with a few side-long glances at Maggie.

"Why are they staring?" said Eenie, shrinking a little behind Julian's leg and clasping at his jeans.

Lee followed their gazes. "It's your hair." Looking around she noticed that no one else had blond or reddish-coloured hair. Most people around them were olive-skinned with dark hair and dark eyes. Edward pulled his hoodie up and Eenie shrunk further behind Julian.

"Let's find a way inside without lining up," Julian murmured. He, too, was uncomfortable at all the attention they were getting.

A high-pitched voice came from behind them. "I know a shortcut!" Turning, they came face to face with a woman they'd never seen before. Or at least, a woman no one had seen before but Lee.

Lee gasped. "You!"

It was the woman in white.

"I didn't mean to scare you," she spoke quickly. "I can help you."

She was pale and odd-looking. Her skin was fair, almost translucent. She wore a long white dress, and her white hair stuck out in tufts all over her head.

"Help us with what?" Edward asked suspiciously.

She turned and fixed him with her dark eyes.

Her eyes look dark, Lee thought, but they're actually very pale. Her pupils are extremely dilated.

"Why, to get into the museum, of course," the woman said, grinning brightly. Her smile exposed a couple of crooked teeth. She was certainly odd, but also seemed quite charming, and Lee could feel the others relax around her. Lee couldn't sense much from her in the way she normally could and wanted to question her more. Julian looked at ease though, so she said nothing.

The woman beckoned to them with a curled finger. She lowered her voice conspiratorially as they grew closer.

"There's a secret entrance into the museum," she said in a low voice.

"Where?" Edward asked with interest.

"I can show you," said the white lady. "Follow me."

The five left the line and followed their pale guide as she navigated them expertly around the concrete wall to a small doorway tucked into the stone, out of sight.

"Through here." She opened the door and led them inside. Though Lee still had her doubts, she could do no more than follow the others as they disappeared inside the walls.

5

The five gasped as they walked through the doorway and into a large room with imposing stone walls. The walls were lined with huge maps, framed by intricately carved wooden panels stretching from floor to ceiling. Small glass cabinets lined the corridors, housing stunning pieces of centuries-old art.

"Look at the ceiling!" Maggie exclaimed.

It was exquisite. It was like looking at a wall of pictures, even more stunning for the fact it was on the ceiling, and everything was rendered in gold. Lee stared open-mouthed at the images of the golden tunnel on the roof, beautiful and shining, stretching out far ahead. Ancient men and women adorned the ceiling as paintings or carvings. Some looked happy, some bemused, others aggressive and fierce.

Edward walked over to the walls to examine the floor-to-ceiling maps. "I don't recognise any of these."

The white lady gave a tinkling laugh. "No, you wouldn't. The men of long ago did not know our world like we know it now."

"Or they're maps of other worlds," Lee said in an undertone to Julian. He shot her a warning glance.

Edward ran his hand over the map's oddly-shaped

continents. "They're huge," he said. "They remind me a bit of our tapestries back home."

Glancing at each other, the same thought occurred to all of them. Was this a clue in their search for the Professor? Their pale guide seemed oblivious to their looks and continued to point out interesting features in her high-pitched voice. Lee waited until the white lady was further ahead and out of earshot before asking Julian in a low voice, "Do you think the Professor was here?"

He pursed his mouth. "I feel like it's a place he would have travelled to. He loved history. Remember that time he spoke all night about the house being built?"

Lee gave a laugh. "Dear old Professor."

"Look around, but be subtle," Julian said in a low voice.

The white lady had gone on ahead and was showing Eenie and Maggie one of the artworks in the glass cabinets. Lee caught sight of a small snow globe in one of the showcases. She mused to herself that it seemed a bit out of place, especially when the gallery was full of magnificent treasures, but shrugged and dismissed it. She walked over to Edward, who was staring somewhat glassy-eyed at the wall. "What are you staring at?"

He turned to her with a small frown, and quietly said, "I swear I recognise that picture." He pointed to the small, expertly framed painting, which was a blur of colours. "I can't see it properly though. It's all blurry."

The painting suddenly detached from the wall and floated neatly into Edward's hand.

Julian had sidled up to them without either one no-ticing. He gave a sheepish shrug in response to their raised eyebrows. Smirking, Edward held up the painting so all three could see it. It was a picture of a hunched old man sitting at a dinner table. His spectacles were smudged, and his white hair was tangled and unkempt.

Lee gave a small squeal.

"Lee, shhhhh!" Edward said, annoyed. The white lady had heard her, and was heading their way, looking curious.

Edward quickly turned the painting into a fraction of its size and stuffed it into his pocket.

"Well, what's happening over here?" the white lady asked in her high-pitched voice.

"Nothing, Lee just stubbed her toe," Julian said quickly. "We should probably get going now. We've used up enough of your time. Thanks so much for helping us cut the line."

The white lady looked a little disappointed. "I can keep showing you around, you know. I've been here many times. I know where the best artworks are."

"That's okay, we've run out of time unfortunately," said Julian as he and the others turned to leave. "Thanks again, though."

The white lady's eyelashes drooped, but she nodded and said goodbye.

* * *

"I feel bad we just ditched her like that," said Maggie after she'd gone. "She was nice."

"I liked her too, but we need to be alone," said Julian. "Edward's found a clue!"

Maggie and Eenie clustered around him in excitement, all else forgotten. Edward withdrew the tiny square from his pocket, and turned it back into the painting. He held it out for the others to see. They stared down at it, then back up at each other, excitedly.

"It's the Professor!" Maggie exclaimed. "But how?"

"Old rogue must have planted it on his travels," Edward said, looking impressed despite himself. Eenie scrabbled in her pocket and withdrew the microphone. "Will this work again?"

"May as well try it," Edward said, holding the painting out towards her.

Eenie held the microphone up. Nothing happened. Seconds went by as five pairs of eyes—two blue, one green, one violet and one grey—stared at the picture, reflecting varying levels of frustration.

"Maybe something else besides the microphone affects it," Lee mused. "Show me the picture again, Edward." He passed it to her.

Lee squinted as she held it closer. "The Professor looks like he's pointing at something."

Edward snatched it from her to peer at it, imitating his sister's frown precisely. He followed the Professor's pointed finger with his eyes, up off the page, to find himself staring at the wall. "It's not pointing at anything,"

"Hang on, try this," said Lee, taking the painting back from Edward, who grunted in annoyance. Lee rotated the painting so the finger pointed the other way, but as she did so, the finger moved, returning to its previous position.

"It's like a compass!" Lee exclaimed. The others looked at her in bewilderment.

"You know what I mean," she said impatiently. "When you move the compass around, the needle points north, so you know which way you need to go! Except maybe this compass doesn't point north. Maybe it points to where *we* need to go."

"Ohh!" Lee's siblings looked excited again. "Follow it, follow it!"

Edward transformed the painting into an intricate, embossed piece of paper, so it looked like they were reading a map rather than staring at a stolen painting. They found it much easier to navigate their way around after that. The Professor's pointed finger led them through galley-ways and doors, until they ended up in a chapel.

"Be careful here," Julian said to them in a low tone. A swarm of people looked upwards in a hushed silence at the majestic god-like depictions painted on the ceiling.

"I think this place is well-known," Lee said to the others. "There are more people here than anywhere else we've seen."

Maggie had the heavy-lidded look that meant she was talking to an animal somewhere. "I think there's a cat in here," she murmured.

"Who cares?" Edward said.

Maggie gave him a small push. "I do! She's frightened with all these people."

Edward flippantly swept his blond fringe from covering his eyes, and shrugged.

Lee glanced around the cavernous room and at the magnificent paintings adorning the ceiling. The figures depicted were in various poses, mostly lounging around or whispering in each other's ears. Some were nude, and some were clothed. Two of the figures were stretching out their hands, touching fingers.

"Wonder if they had powers back then," Edward mused, following her gaze. "Kind of reminds me of when our palms touch."

"This way," Julian called to them, holding the pointing Professor.

They followed him through to the next room, its walls also bedecked with large and complex artworks.

"Julian!" Lee elbowed him hard in the ribs.

"Ooof! WHAT?!"

"LOOK!"

The painting at which Lee was pointing depicted an animal against a completely white backdrop. It was stark and ugly, not only due to the jagged brush strokes and dull colours, but the image itself. Something about the image of the animal made Julian come to a sudden and complete standstill.

"No!" he said in a hushed voice.

The others made low, almost growl-like noises as they approached the picture and stood next to Julian. Eenie looked at her siblings curiously, one by one, before turning to stare at the picture.

"How is it possible?" Lee looked at Julian, wide-eyed.

"It can't be!" Maggie exclaimed. "They've obviously been around for a long time," Edward mused. "Everything in this museum is ancient."

Julian ushered them all away quickly. "Come on, people are looking," he said. He was right—clusters of tourists were intrigued by whatever painting had so interested the small group of excited children, and were on their way over to it.

As the other children moved away, Julian had to pull Eenie with him. She was transfixed by the image of the huge black horse, its shadowy eyes glowering menacingly under the stubby horn protruding from its forehead. Her eyes, once a bright blue, were now a stormy, dark colour. As Julian guided her away, the crowd around them parted. Eenie's expression had them drawing back, as if they were strangely apprehensive of the small child.

They followed the Professor's outstretched hand once more, navigating their way through several more rooms. Maggie drew their attention to an enormous mural that adorned an entire wall. There were seats in front of it for people to sit and have their picture taken.

"Wow, that's huge," she said wonderingly.

"I think it's famous," said Edward.

"Why? It's just a picture of people about to eat, isn't it?

"Sounds good enough to me to be famous!" Edward grinned.

"Why are they all sitting on one side of the table?" Maggie said.

Edward rolled his eyes. "So, the painter could get them all in, duh!"

Two people nearby turned at their words, a handsome young man and pretty young woman with her long hair tied up in a messy top knot.

"We said almost the exact same thing, didn't we, Milly?" The young man laughed, his dark brown hair falling carelessly over his glasses.

Facing the children with an infectious smile, the young woman said, "We think the painter was trying to tell us some interesting secret! They say the bread rolls on the dinner table correspond to musical notes."

The five grinned at this, captivated by her smile.

She grinned back. "I know, it is a bit daft isn't it?" She intertwined one of her arms with one of the young man's, and told the five, "Another great artwork here is the sunflowers, if you get a chance to see them."

"Unfortunately we're short on time," Julian explained politely.

"Oh, that's a shame. Maybe next time then." The young woman waved merrily at them as she and the young man walked excitedly to the next painting.

The group followed the Professor's pointing finger into the next room.

"This is interesting," Maggie said, looking at a big marble plaque. "In the ancient folklore of this area, women were burnt at the stake for practising witchcraft. They often had familiars—mystical creatures that took the form of small animals or birds and would assist them with their magic.'"

"You wouldn't have lasted long in that era, Maggie!" Edward said playfully, ruffling his sister's hair.

She laughed. "Not at all!"

"Look who it is," Julian said, pushing his chin out. They turned.

The white lady was standing in the corner of the room, peering owlishly at one of the paintings. Catching sight of the group, she waved enthusiastically and started to walk over.

"Edward, the paper!" hissed Lee. He hastily put the embossed sheet back in his pocket.

"Well! How lovely to run into each other again," she trilled, beaming at the group. Lee was struck again by how odd she looked. Not only were her tufted hair and dress white, even her shoes were patent white brogues, and her long nails were painted in a muted, colourless shade. Sidelong glances from other people in the room confirmed her eccentricity.

"You have big earrings!" Eenie stated in the loud and obvious tone of the very young.

The white lady smiled down at her and swung her head

from side to side, causing two white snowflakes to swing madly from her earlobes. "Thank you, dear, how nice of you to say!" Her voice echoed around the room. She crouched down next to Eenie and took one earring out to show her.

Julian hastily whispered to the others. "Should we invite her to lunch? I feel a bit bad for ditching her earlier when she'd been so helpful."

The others were in agreement.

"Uh, excuse me," said Julian as the white lady stood up and put her earring back in place. "Would you like to join us for lunch?"

The white lady responded with an over-the-top, "Oh, how WONDERFUL! Oh, LUNCH! Yes, LET'S!" People who hadn't been staring before now turned to gape at their group.

"Geez," mumbled Edward.

Julian rapidly ushered them towards the cafeteria on the third floor, already regretting his decision.

6

They soon found a good spot—a small, cosy round table with a checkered tablecloth and a tiny vase containing a single plastic flower. A harried-looking waitress dumped a basket of breadsticks and a pitcher of water on the table, telling them curtly to order at the register.

After they had ordered, the white lady kept drawing attention to them with her shrill cries of delight. "Oh, your EYES!" she exclaimed, staring into Lee's. Lee shifted uncomfortably under her intense gaze.

"Most people have them," Edward muttered.

She turned to fix her big pupils on him. "Not that GREEN though!" She squinted at Edward. Moving closer to him, she peered at him again.

He recoiled slightly. She didn't seem to pick up on the hint and kept staring at him, clapping her hands together in a sudden movement.

"Look at your mischievous face! How GORGEOUS! Aren't you handsome!" she trilled. Edward turned an interesting shade of pink and shoveled more bread into his mouth. Lee noticed he didn't move again though, and even appeared to be hiding a slight smile.

The white lady placed her hand on Julian's arm and

laughed as he made his usual serious remarks. "You're such a SOLEMN boy!"

"I'm not a boy," Julian said, puffing his chest out a little.

"Oh, of course you're not!" she said, smiling. "You're a young man. So very tall too." Julian's chest puffed out even further.

Lee quirked an eyebrow at her brothers. Her sisters seemed to be finding the white lady less annoying and more charming as time went on.

Eenie was spellbound, sitting and gazing at the white lady with an adoring expression as she showed them all the various diamond rings on her fingers. Maggie talked to her about the cat she'd met at the museum, and the white lady's pupils dilated even more as she avidly nodded along.

They'd ordered a few different types of food to share. Soon, the table was covered with custard pastries dotted with raisins, a large steaming margharita pizza and a big bowl of fettucine carbonara with garlic bread. There was silence as they all tucked in, enjoying the food too much to talk.

* * *

"Oh, but you should have SEEN it!" the white lady cried, finishing a tale that left them in stitches of laughter as they consumed the last of the food.

"That was amazing," Edward said, still chewing. He

slumped in his chair with a groan. The plates now contained nothing more than a few scattered crumbs.

Edward leaned further back in his chair and put his hand in his pocket. Staring at Lee, he blinked rapidly as he felt around. With a frantic gesture, he searched his other pocket. He brought the chair up with a sharp snap and turned to Julian, face white. Lee pinched him quickly before he blurted out what she knew he was about to say.

"Why don't you show Eenie that artwork you told us about before?" Lee said quickly to the white lady.

"Good idea!" Maggie had picked up what was going on. "I'll come with you," she said cheerily to the white lady, ushering her and Eenie out of the cafeteria, with a nod to Lee as they left.

"You didn't," Lee hissed at Edward.

"It's not there!" Edward said in a strangled voice.

"Are you serious? How could you lose it?" Julian said harshly.

"I don't know!" Edward exclaimed. "It was a piece of paper! It must have fallen out somewhere."

They looked around the cafeteria, peering under the table and scanning the floor surrounding them. After the fifth time Lee asked Edward to check his pockets, he said something cutting under his breath and stalked off.

"The white lady's coming back," Julian said, with a side glance towards the cafeteria entrance. The lady, Eenie and Maggie were laughing cheerily as they approached the table.

Lee's keen eye spotted it right away.

Maggie dropped into the seat next to her, the intricate, embossed piece of paper in hand. Grinning, she placed it at the centre of the table. "Look what the white lady found in the next gallery!"

"I thought I saw you all consulting a map before!" the white lady trilled happily. "I have good eyes. I saw it on the floor and gave it to Maggie."

"Edward will be pleased," said Julian, relief clear in his voice.

They looked around for him, but he'd left the cafeteria.

"We'll find him," said Lee, shifting in her seat, resisting the urge to roll her eyes.

Julian paid for lunch, insisting over the white lady's protestations that it was their treat, and thanked her again for being so helpful.

After she'd bid the group farewell, they went looking for Edward.

"Oh, he's a pain," said Julian after they left the fourth room they'd searched with no sign of him. They were milling around in one of the Renaissance art rooms when suddenly an overhead alarm went off with a loud wail. *WHOOP-WHOOP-WHOOP!* A loud electronic voice boomed out, ordering people to head to the nearest exit.

The sound of running feet indicated people were quickly making their escape.

"Hold on to each other!" Julian called as the people around them surged towards the doorway. The girls held onto each other's arms as they were caught up in the crushing crowd. Lee felt like a sheep being herded as they were directed towards each exit by burly security guards, barking orders. She noticed Julian keeping a close eye on the younger girls, and she followed his lead, making sure their little sisters were enveloped between the two of them as they exited the building.

None of the lifts could be taken, so they joined the ever-swelling, surging crowd taking the stairs. The stairwell was soon swarming with people, and Lee started to sway a little with the press of people all around.

"Lee, try to focus on one thing," Julian said, catching sight of her pale, tense face.

Lee blinked rapidly at the onslaught of the crowd's pressing urge to escape from the building. She couldn't let their thoughts overwhelm her now; Eenie and Maggie were relying on her and Julian to get them out safely. She swore all kinds of things mentally at Edward, then gritted her teeth and tried to concentrate.

Eenie and Maggie gripped arms tightly as the crowd pushed and swayed against them. The stairwell seemed to go on forever: endless stone stairs, going down, down, down.

After what seemed like an eternity to Lee, but was only moments later, they finally descended the last of the stair-wells. They surged out with the teeming crowd into the cooling, late afternoon air. Julian shepherded them quickly to one side, and they huddled together in a small group, away from everyone else.

Lee stood with eyes closed, breeze cool on her flushed face, and waited for her beating heart to slow down.

"How are we going to find Edward now?" Maggie cried.

Julian and Lee glanced at each other, a little lost. No one said anything. Eenie slipped her hand into Lee's in the silence. Her palm twinged, the usual sensation she experienced when her palm touched one of her siblings'.

Glancing at her other hand, she said, almost absently, "Why don't we try the five-as-one power?"

"There're only four of us, though," Maggie noted.

Julian pursed his lips. "We've never tried it with one of us missing, but it might just work." The others didn't take much convincing, as they'd all been curious to try out their combined powers again.

"Let's get away from this crowd first," said Julian. He led them away from the noisy press of people talking excitedly amongst themselves about the evacuation.

The four of them walked on until they came across a sprawling mass of old ruins. There were still a few people milling around, remnants of the heavy crowd that had burst out of the museum like sheep from a corral. The crumbling structures were massive, and scattered across the grounds, providing a good cover. It was an impressive and fascinating array of ruins whispering tales of the glorious ancient past.

Lee glanced around. "This place is pretty cool." The wreckage of what had once been an earlier city still cast a striking and arresting view. Tall pillars, crumbling gates and ancient stone buttresses exuded the eerie and mystical feel of a culture long gone.

They formed a small circle near one of the pillars and held each other's hands. There was silence as they stood with their heads slightly bowed. The silence started to grow heavy and eventually felt strained as they continued to stand there with nothing happening. One by one, they glanced up at Julian, who waved at them to try again.

Still nothing.

"Try to concentrate really hard on Edward," Julian suggested, shaking his hands slightly, still holding onto his sisters'. Lee's and Maggie's arms shook from the action. The group was silent as they concentrated.

Still nothing.

"All that's happening is my palms are burning," said Lee. She let go of Eenie's hand and rubbed her palm on her leg.

"Mine too," Julian said somewhat reluctantly, letting go as well.

"How are we going to find Edward?" Maggie asked, her voice catching.

The familiar crease appeared between Julian's eyebrows as he looked unseeingly at the ancient ruins around them.

Eenie looked at Maggie's worried expression and reached for Lee's hand again. "I can find Edward!" she said eagerly.

"It's okay, Eenie, we'll just have to look for him," Lee said, trying to reassure her.

"But I can find him!" she said, firmness in her voice. "I

need your powers to do it." She stuck her small hand up, demanding Lee take it.

Lee laughed at her determined little face and went along with it. "Okay," she said, putting her hand in Eenie's.

With a sudden roar in her ears, and a rush like she was being hurtled through space, she found herself in a vision.

. . . Edward was wandering the cobbled streets, looking anxious and a little fearful. He'd never meant to lose the others . . .

. . . He'd wandered off to the next room in a huff and found himself in a sudden evacuation, being pushed out onto the streets with a crowd of strangers . . .

. . . He hunched his shoulders as he wandered over to a line of shopfronts . . .

. . . Edward gazed up at a sign that declared CAFFE DEPALO in shiny black letters . . ."

"He's at a café!"

Lee came to, ears still roaring. She yelled at Julian, "He's at a place called Café Depalo! I'll explain later!" She sprinted off. Julian called out something after her, but picked up Eenie and ran in her wake, Maggie on his heels. Lee kept yelling out directions as they made a run for it out of the ruins.

"Follow me down this street!" Lee cried over her shoulder, making a beeline for the cobbled footpath in the distance. With the vision fading each second, she ran down the paved path, searching urgently at the top of the shopfronts for the shiny black sign.

"EDWARD! EDWAAAAARD!!"

There he was.

He had just been about to walk away from the café and off elsewhere down the street. Lee had just made it in time. He turned at her voice, relief flooding his face, and sprinted towards his sister.

"LEE!"

They collided in a big hug, and spoke over the top of each other, words tumbling as their relief flooded over them.

"How did you find me?"

"We found you!"

"Thank goodness you're here!"

"I was beginning to get so worried!"

"The alarm went off and I got evacuated!"

"We were trying to look for you when it happened!"

"I didn't mean to lose you!"

Julian finally caught up to them, panting hard from the effort of carrying Eenie. He put her down, too winded to speak, and waved in relief at Edward as he clutched his side. Maggie was close behind and ran straight towards Edward.

"You're here! Where have you been? Why did you run off?" Her garbled voice was lost in Edward's jumper as she hugged him tightly. He grinned and pulled his sister closer, too relieved to say anything else.

7

"I was kicking myself for leaving you!" Edward said. They were seated at a small restaurant, a few hours later, the excitement still evident in their voices and faces as they talked. The five sipped hot chocolates in the cooling afternoon as the last of the sun's rays started to disappear.

"Why did you leave anyway?" said Lee, scooping up a marshmallow bobbing in her drink.

"I didn't mean to leave you all for long." Edward at least had the grace to look shamefaced. "I just needed a walk to cool off. You were pestering me!" He frowned at Lee.

She shook her head. "Still, stupid of you to wander off!"

"I know," Edward muttered. "I won't do it again." This last statement was directed at Julian, who hadn't said much.

Julian nodded. "I'll speak to you about it later," he said with a short glance at his brother, then turned to help Eenie with her marshmallows.

"I'm in trouble." Edward spoke with his usual bravado, but his bottom lip shook slightly.

"Of course you are," said Lee in clipped tones. Seeing his expression, her face softened slightly, and she put a few more marshmallows into his mug.

"So how did you find me?" Edward said, holding the

marshmallows down with his spoon so they softened in the creamy chocolate.

"Eenie actually did it!" Lee said, smiling at their youngest sister. "Her powers did something to mine. I'm not sure what exactly." Lee paused, remembering. "But she put me into a vision!" she finished triumphantly.

"Wow, that's pretty neat!" Edward said, impressed. He grinned at his little sister, whose cheeks were slowly turning pink. "Good one, Eenie!"

"It was SUCH a great experience actually!" Lee went on. "I've never been able to control my visions, so it was awesome to be able to see something *I* wanted to see for once!" She was almost more excited than she'd been when they'd found Edward. "The vision was obviously just a few minutes into the future too, because you were about to leave as soon as we got to you."

"Very helpful!" Maggie chimed in.

"You did well Eenie, good work!" Julian smiled down at her. Dimples flashing, she ducked her head and pulled her mug towards her.

"I've still lost our paper though," said Edward, looking shamefaced again. "I'm not doing very well right now, am I?'

Julian socked him on the arm. "Nothing new there." Edward snorted and socked him back.

In all the excitement, they'd completely forgotten about the piece of paper. "Here it is, you clown," Maggie said, drawing the intricate, embossed paper out of her pocket.

"We found it after you stormed off."

Edward blew out a sigh. "Thank goodness." He took it from her and opened it up. Seeing his shocked expression, Lee took it from him and looked at it. It was blank.

"Whaaa . . ." Edward said, snatching it off her and flipping it furiously over and over again.

"Where'd the painting go?" Lee said.

"What are you talking about?" Maggie said. She took it from Edward and did the same motion, flipping it back to front like something would magically appear.

Edward took it again and shook it a little, turning it over.

"It's definitely blank," Julian said.

"Maybe it went blank because Edward wasn't carrying it," said Lee.

"Maybe," said Julian.

"His powers transformed the painting in the first place," Maggie agreed.

"It's definitely our map though; I recognise the paper I turned it into." Edward traced the embossed, glossy paper.

"Could your powers have worn off?" Lee speculated.

"Maybe it's blank because we're no longer in the museum," said Julian.

"Oh, well, the map part of it has disappeared now, whatever the reason," said Edward, shoulders slumping.

Eenie piped up, changing the subject. "I'm hungry!" The sun was sinking on the horizon and seemed to punctuate her words with the last of its rays. It had turned a deep purple against the grey sky, which soon transformed into a glorious crimson red with gold, purple and blue hues. The group was silent for a few moments, watching the sunset in all its splendour.

"Let's order some food then," Julian said finally. He took charge and caught the hovering waiter's eye. The waiter passed around menus, and they didn't take long to decide on their orders of pizza, pasta and gelati. Soon the sounds of clinking silverware against porcelain was all that could be heard.

Maggie broke the silence by singing, "Mary, Mary, quite contrary."

Edward chuckled and sang the next line. "How does your garden grow?"

"With silver bells and cockle shells," sang Lee.

"And one lousy little petunia!" Eenie chimed in, ending the song unexpectedly. They laughed, turning the heads of the other patrons.

As they kept eating, Lee thought she heard a faint miaow nearby. She glanced around and noticed Maggie's heavy-lidded eyes as she stared off into the distance.

Catching Lee's eye, she raised her eyebrows and, with one shoulder, indicated towards Julian. Knowing what her sister was about to say, Lee gave a tiny nod with unspoken acknowledgement that she'd back her up.

"Juliaaaaan," Maggie wheedled.

"What?"

"The cat from the museum is here."

He spared her a brief glance and sighed.

"Julian, she's scared, and the crowds almost trampled her!"

"We should help her then," Lee said, smiling in return to Maggie's grateful glance.

"She wants to come with us," Maggie said in the same wheedling voice. Julian sighed again.

Another miaow sounded, this time closer, and Lee watched as a scruffy white blur darted under their table. She picked up a corner of the tablecloth and peered underneath. A small, grubby and dishevelled bundle sat gracefully against a table leg. The cat's tail was wrapped around herself in a tight, curling knot, and her eyes shone like laser beams as she stared back at Lee.

Unwrapping herself in one slinky motion, the cat sauntered over to Lee's outstretched fingers, surveying them down her nose. She took one delicate sniff, and then walked straight past, blatantly ignoring her. Somewhat disgruntled, Lee sat back up and watched as the cat padded over to Maggie and butted her small head against her sister's leg.

Maggie looked down fondly at the small white cat. Her white tail curled up into the air like a wisp of smoke. "She wants to come with us," she said again, with a beseeching look at Julian.

He shrugged and nodded half-heartedly. "As long as she doesn't get in the way."

"She won't," said Maggie happily. It was part of the groups normal way of things, to have some small animal or creature follow Maggie. Although she was dirty in patches, the cat had lustrous, snowy-white fur. Her appearance was very unusual; she had one brown eye and one blue. Edward made fun of her, pointing out her mismatched eyes and funny little chopstick legs, until the cat stretched out a small paw and stuck claws like tiny pins into his arm. He left her alone after that. Maggie named the cat 'Chopsticks' with a gleam in her eye.

They tucked into their meal, although a substantial portion of Maggie's went under the table. Street sellers with flowers kept coming up to the table asking if they wanted to buy some, but Julian shooed them away.

"Try not to catch their eye, Maggie," Julian said as the fifth one approached their table. Maggie smiled at the vendor apologetically. "I feel sorry for them," she said. "The flowers are beautiful too."

"I can make you a flower anytime, Maggie!" said Edward, licking cheese off his finger. He took a piece of coiled pasta from the bowl in front of him and, with a flourish, handed Maggie a curling daffodil.

She promptly ate it, much to Edward's disgust. "Still tastes like pasta! Lazy!"

He gave a sheepish laugh and raised a shoulder. "In my defence, you weren't supposed to eat it!"

Lee asked the question foremost in all of their minds. "How do we know where to go next?"

"What about the book?" Maggie suddenly asked.

The book! Lee had completely forgotten about it. Taking

it out of her backpack, she waved it at the others. "I forgot to tell you I accidentally opened it back at the house."

"What?" Julian exclaimed. "What did it say?"

"I was in a rush," Lee said. "I just saw it long enough to see it was a message from our parents."

Julian tilted his head. "It did that to me once as well. It made no sense at the time."

"Did it make sense later?"

Julian nodded, the skin around his eyes crinkling almost imperceptibly. "See what it says," he said huskily.

Lee breathed deeply and put her palm on the cover of the book. The swirl twisted and turned, and five beams of light rose to connect with the birthmarks on Lee's palm. The light pierced the skin and disappeared, leaving Lee with a slight burning sensation.

The book flicked its pages in the usual way before opening to a page about halfway. Everyone bent over it. Edward's impatience got the better of him, and he grabbed the book from Lee's hands. He snorted as he peered down at the page.

"There's nothing there!"

Lee snatched it back off him. "It was my message. Maybe I'm the only one who should be reading it!"

The book sent its pages into a wild spin at her words.

Lee laughed and wrinkled her nose at Edward. "See?" He rolled his eyes and made a rude gesture back.

She gripped the book firmly and opened it again. This time, the writing had reappeared.

"To our darling Lee.
If you are reading this, the book has deemed you ready
to read our words to you."

Lee pulled the book closer and read the next sentence carefully.

Lee, our daughter. Mind the wrath, the poison hath.
We are so proud of all of you.
Yours,
Amelia and Mike Delliks.

Lee frowned at the page in confusion.

Julian gave a resigned laugh at her expression. "It was the same with me," he said. "It'll make sense at some point."

Lee exhaled noisily, shoving the book into her backpack.

"Ooooh, look!" said Eenie, through a mouthful of pizza. She pointed down the cobbled pathway. Standing a few metres away was a man dressed all in silver, standing as still as a statue, with a small suitcase open on the ground before him. The five watched as passers-by dropped coins into his case. Each time, he would move and perform a small dance or strike a cheeky pose.

"Watch me," Edward said to the others. He scooted his chair back with a screeching sound of metal on cobbled pavement.

Ignoring Julian and Lee's cries of "Edward!" and "Ed,

don't!", he made his way over to the performer. He picked up a couple of stray stones along the way, sneakily transforming them into bright orange balls.

Lee couldn't be bothered admonishing him further, and sat back in her chair with a small shake of her head, lips twitching.

Edward sidled up behind the performer and started to expertly juggle three balls as the performer did another small dance. People nearby caught sight of the double act and started to wander over to watch. The performer had no idea Edward was behind him and grew more animated in front of the growing audience.

"Such a show-off," Julian said, half amused, half exasperated.

"You should teach him a lesson," Lee murmured.

Julian started muttering something about not using their powers in public, but his words were lost as the audience burst into laughter. Edward was now deftly juggling four orange balls, and a banana had somehow made its way into the whirling storm. The orange and yellow blurs spun in the air, while the duped street performer continued his little act, still completely unaware the audience wasn't for him.

Lee felt Julian shift beside her. Suddenly the orange balls and banana stopped mid-air and hovered around Edward's ears. Edward tried to snatch them out of the air, but to no avail. The banana gave his nose a sharp rap and then stayed poised there, making him look like a seal balancing a ball. Edward tried to swat it away, but it didn't budge.

The audience, of course, thought this was part of the act, and roared in laughter.

Edward made a last futile attempt at grabbing the balls, but they simply boxed him around the ears and stayed hovering just out of reach. Edward shot their table a glare and eventually gave up, giving the crowd an exaggerated bow farewell. They had loved it and showed it with whistles and cheers. The street performer was grinning widely, thinking he was doing a fantastic job.

"Subtle," Edward grumbled as he came back to their table.

"Says you!" Lee said, with a wide grin, having thoroughly enjoyed the spectacle. Maggie and Eenie were giggling into their napkins. Julian just smirked at his brother as Edward sulkily snatched up a bread roll.

When it came time to pay the bill, Julian fished a few notes out and left it in the leather billfold.

"What have we been doing for money this whole time?" Lee asked, the thought suddenly striking her. Julian looked a bit guilty and glanced quickly at Edward, who held up a couple of napkins.

"Oh!" Lee gave a small snort of laughter. Edward smiled and gave her a lazy wink.

"It's getting late, and we don't know what our next move is," said Julian. "How about we find somewhere to stay for the night and start again in the morning?"

Edward handed him some more magically transformed

napkins, which Julian used to pay for a hotel for the night. Lee noticed the more money there was, the less they were asked questions about where their parents were.

Although, she mused, that seems to be happening less frequently than usual anyway. Julian's voice had deepened since they'd first arrived at the Professor's house, and she'd noticed his shoulders were getting broader too. Since they had started their new expedition, his confidence seemed to have increased also, and his natural air of authority was making more of an impression with adults.

That's come in handy, Lee thought, smiling to herself as they were courteously shown to their hotel suite.

8

The next morning, the group came down to a big continental breakfast. Platters of cold meats, cheeses and assorted breads, and large glass jugs of orange juice sat on the dining table.

"How are we going to figure out where to go to next?" Lee asked, helping herself to some crusty rolls.

"Well, Mr Lennon said we had to retrace the Professor's travels," Maggie reminded them.

"I've been thinking . . ." Julian said, pursing his lips.

"I wondered what that noise was," Edward smirked. The toast heading towards his mouth suddenly slipped from his hand and fell with a thud on the table. Edward bit down on thin air. "Hey!" he exclaimed.

"As I was saying," Julian continued, ignoring his brother, "I've been thinking about the bicorn painting we saw in the museum."

He was referring to the black horse with the stubby horn that had captured all their attention immediately. The bicorn was a sinister creature they'd encountered on their last adventures and finding a painting of it so casually in a public place, was disconcerting to them all.

"Mediarn's animal," Maggie said with a small shiver.

Eenie shifted suddenly in her seat, upturning a plate of eggs all over the floor.

Julian quickly cleaned it up and got his sister another breakfast.

"What about it?" Lee said as they continued eating.

"To see it in the musuem, after all our previous encounters with it," said Julian. Eenie's eyes grew stormy but no one noticed, engrossed as they were in the conversation.

"It seems like a pretty big coincidence," said Julian. "The Professor ended up capturing one of them remember."

"How docs that help us now though?" Lee asked.

"Well, think about it," Julian said, reaching for more ham. "If the Professor travelled through here and saw the same painting, maybe he went searching for a bicorn."

"I still don't see how that helps us now, though," Lee said. "All the bicorns are gone after we had the final battle with Mediarn. Thanks to you." She added the last sentence almost as an afterthought to her brother. Julian raised his shoulder, flushing a little. No one had noticed Eenie's unnatural stillness throughout the conversation.

Maggie slowly nodded. "Oh, I see! It's the clue that will lead us to his next destination." She quickly snuck a few pieces of cold meat into her over-sized shoulder bag, which started to purr.

"Exactly," Julian said, pleased.

"Seems a bit loose," Edward remarked.

Julian shrugged. "Any other ideas then?"

They looked around at each other, the silence broken

only by Maggie enthusiastically slurping her orange juice.

"Actually . . ." Lee said, her brow furrowing slightly. "Remember how we first read about the bicorns in that history book at the house?"

The others nodded.

"The chapters were on Ancient Roman and Egyptian culture," she said, raising her eyebrows quizzically.

"Oh!" Julian and Edward said simultaneously.

"Egypt . . ." Lee trailed off.

"Makes sense, since we've spotted a trace of them here," said Edward. He stood up, causing his chair to fall backwards. "Let's go!"

Julian smiled and mopped up the puddle of orange juice in front of Eenie with a napkin.

"Hold on," he said to Edward. "Let's finish breakfast first."

Edward shrugged with impatience, but sat back down. Jamming a slice of cheese into his mouth, he turned to Maggie. "Can your birds help us again?"

Maggie looked surprised. "I thought you said they were ugly?"

"They are," Edward said with his mouth full. "Doesn't mean they can't help us though!"

Maggie rolled her eyes. "I'll try to find one to help us. With any luck, they'll still be nearby." Maggie left the dining room, whispering a few soothing words into her bag.

"Should we take some supplies with us?" Lee asked. "The food Edward transforms always tastes like the object he's changed it from!"

"Not ideal when there will probably only be sand around," agreed Edward, refusing to take the bait.

"Good idea, Lee," Julian said. "Take what you can from the buffet table. Don't be obvious though!" he said as Edward jumped up to help. They didn't take long and came back with bulging pockets and enormous napkin-covered parcels.

"This will keep us going for a while!" Edward said gleefully. "I'll make us an extra backpack out of this," he said, taking a thick linen napkin from the table.

"Not here," Julian said, glancing around. "We're becoming a bit careless with using our powers in public lately."

"Although no one's really here," Lee said, looking over at the only people in the room, an elderly couple.

Maggie came into the dining room moments after Edward left. "I found one of our ibises that came with us before!" she told them breathlessly.

"I told him where we want to go, and he says that's one of their old family homes." She pulled out one of the chairs and perched on the edge. "It will be no problem to take us there!"

"Great!" Julian said, pleased.

Edward soon came back to the table with a white linen backpack.

"Very pretty," said Lee teasingly, opening the gold-threaded flap.

"Yeah, yeah," Edward muttered, turning crimson. "I had to make do with what I had."

"Let's get going," Julian said once they'd packed it to the brim. "Come on, Eenie." He held his little sister's hand and led her out of the dining room, the others in tow.

* * *

The Delliks siblings headed out into the fresh morning air, back to the spot where they'd left the bathtub. The area was deserted and the bathtub looked untouched. The white porcelain was grubby from their previous flight, and they got in gingerly, trying not to rub up against the dirty sides.

Maggie stroked the ibis's snowy plumage as he perched on the edge of the tub. His partially webbed feet clutched the rim while his kindly black eyes blinked at them.

"Why is he bald?" Eenie said in her little voice, staring up at the bird curiously as she sat huddled in the bathtub.

"Because it helps him fly faster," Maggie said fondly, stroking her finger down the bird's long, graceful neck. She carefully placed her bag in the bathtub with a few crooning words. The bag gave a low purr.

Julian and Maggie glanced at each other in silent acknowledgement. The bathtub started to rise slowly as the ibis gave a throaty croak and launched himself off the rim. He flapped his wings lazily to stay afloat alongside them as the bathtub rose into the sky, faster and faster, until they were miles above the earth. The protective cocoon that seemed to surround their tub once again protected them from the elements. More throaty croaks surrounded them as a dozen or so other ibises joined them.

They flew like a shooting arrow over the vast sprawl of Rome, leaving the majestic city behind. Peering over the rim of the tub, wind whistling around their ears, they watched the puffy, cotton wool clouds sail past them.

Lee thought anyone looking up in the sky at that moment would have thought they'd gone completely mad. Maggie stayed quiet as she chattered to the birds in her mind, only occasionally speaking out loud to give Julian directions.

Lee sank further into the cushioned tub and watched as Eenie sat curled in Julian's lap, eyes bright blue as she gripped the bathtub's edges. Edward and Maggie played paper, scissors, rock. Maggie gave a cute squeal of delight every time she beat her brother. *Which is impressively often*, Lee thought, smiling in enjoyment as she watched Edward get continually beaten by his younger sister. Edward eventually threw his hands up. "You win, you win!" Maggie grinned and sat back in triumph. Her laugh was lost to the wind as they shot through the sky following the flying ibises v-formation.

* * *

"Happy Birthday, Lee!" they all chorused the next morning. They had navigated quite quickly the previous day thanks to Maggie's ibis. When they'd arrived on the outskirts of the desert, Edward had conjured up a tent for them all out of Maggie's sock. After a hurried dinner, they'd fallen asleep quickly, not even noticing that the tent still had the hole from Maggie's toe.

Lee beamed and listened to them sing Happy Birthday. "Thank you!" she said happily.

Julian suggested they eat breakfast outside the tent, and they sat cross-legged on a large rug, provided thanks to Edward's inventiveness by another napkin.

"Oops," said Edward, moving his foot to reveal a large rip in the rug. "I couldn't make it very thick, unfortunately."

"It works well enough," Julian said as he passed around breakfast rolls.

Maggie fed small morsels to Chopsticks, who was looking decidedly grumpy at the sand blowing over her fur. After daintily snatching the food until she'd had her fill, she stalked off, tail high in the air, back into the tent.

Sitting in contented silence, Lee gazed around at their surroundings. She hadn't paid much attention when they'd arrived the night before; the only thing on her mind had been impatience as she'd waited for Edward to make her a bed out of an ibis feather.

They were surrounded by dusty, golden sand as far as the eye could see. The only things that broke up the monotony were large peaked dunes that rose in smooth mounds over the plains. The air was hot and dry, and the sand from the dunes blew lightly over them as they munched away.

"Me first," Edward said once they'd finished breakfast. The five had a tradition where they used their powers to create each other's birthday gifts. Julian had started it when they were small—a tradition he remembered doing with their parents when they were still alive.

Edward dropped a large parcel into Lee's lap. She opened it to reveal a yellow beaded bracelet clearly made from grains of sands.

"Very clever!" Lee laughed, putting it on her wrist.

"Tell me something I don't know!" Edward said, waggling his eyebrows.

"Waterfall is the opposite of firefly."

Edward opened his mouth then closed it. Lee laughed again, in high spirits, and stuck her tongue out at him.

Maggie looked a bit shamefaced as she passed Lee a large box of strawberries.

"Sorry, I was concentrating on getting us here and didn't think about your present enough. The birds helped me find these."

"Getting us here was present enough!" Lee hugged her. "And these look delicious." She doled out the fat, pink strawberries to the others.

Eenie was next and handed Lee a small parcel. She tore open the wrappings to reveal a small white bag. It was beaded and had small, sparkly, silver threads running through it. Lee thought it was beautiful and said as much to Eenie.

"Julian helped me pick it out at the museum gift shop," Eenie explained, looking pleased at Lee's reaction. "There's something inside."

Lee opened the bag and saw a tiny white purse fitting snugly within it. She took it out and opened it. There was a gold ring inside. She paused, unsure how it related to Eenie's powers.

"Is it okay?" asked Eenie with the tiniest of a quiver in her voice.

Julian added quickly, "It's to help channel your powers."

The Professor showed me that the gold coin helped me focus my power, Lee suddenly remembered. "Oh, of course!" she exclaimed, touched. "That's a fantastic present, Eenie!" Her little sister beamed back at her.

Julian stood up with a flourish and gestured for Lee to follow him for his present. He climbed up to the peak of a nearby sand dune and stood at the top with his eyes closed. Lee, walking behind him, found the rolling motion of the sand beneath her feet soothing. *It's a pleasant change walking on this after the cobbled streets of a city,* she thought abstractly. She gazed at the vast yellow terrain around her and marvelled at the sight. She really hadn't seen anything like it before. They were glorious, the rolling patterns over the dunes, decorated by sandy whorls and swirls.

They all watched their older brother with an expectant air. Slowly, the tiny grains of sand on the dune rolled downward.

"Wow!" Edward said as the dune continued to shift and tilt until the sand was rolling down it like a huge sandy slide.

"Come on, it's supposed to be fun!" Julian said with a grin, seeing Lee's startled expression.

Edward needed no further encouragement and yelled in delight. With a flying leap he jumped on the sandy slide. His roars of laughter echoed across the dunes as he shot down to the bottom.

Surprisingly, Eenie ran to the slide just as fearlessly as Edward. She launched her tiny self at the rolling sand, and screamed delightedly, her hair flying out like yellow streamers as she followed Edward.

With a reluctant grin at Julian's urging, Lee made her way over to the gushing sand. Taking a deep breath, she sat on the edge and pushed herself off onto the moving grit. Lee's vision blurred as she flew down the slope. Landing in an ungraceful heap at the bottom, she couldn't stop giggling. Edward was grinning madly as he helped haul her to her feet.

"Look, here comes Maggie!" he cried, shading his eyes with his hand.

Maggie's screams of delight reached their ears as she hurtled down the slope, chortling with glee and landing much more gracefully than Lee. Brushing the sand off, she and Edward exclaimed over each other excitedly about how much fun it had been.

A yell sounded down to them. Turning, the four looked up at Julian on the top of the dune. He raised his hands. The sliding, gushing sand halted suddenly. The group watched in awe as it slowly started to climb back uphill.

Julian yelled something to them again, but it was unintelligible.

"I think we can go back up again!" Edward exclaimed. He gingerly stepped onto the churning grit and gave a half-excited, half-fearful shriek as the sand caught him and swept him off his feet. He was taken swiftly uphill, bellowing something to the others in between loud bursts of laughter.

"May as well!" Maggie said. She held her hand out to Eenie, but the little girl shook her head, grinning, and launched herself on her own onto the sandy slide. She gave a delighted scream, and Maggie and Lee watched as she flew uphill on the rolling sands, giggling the whole way.

"She's getting far too bold," Maggie smiled.

"We're probably not the best influences," Lee said, raising one eyebrow while watching her little sister's tiny, retreating body.

"She's having nightmares though," Maggie whispered.

Lee turned to face her. "What do you mean?"

"I think it must be from her kidnapping," Maggie explained, turning her face away to look at their little sister, now giving her brothers high fives. Maggie's shoulders hunched a little. "She wakes up crying and talks about a big face looming over her."

Lee sighed and closed her eyes. "Why haven't I noticed?"

Maggie's lips twisted. "She made me promise not to tell. She didn't want anyone else to know about it."

Lee opened her eyes and smiled at her sister. "I can understand that. I won't say anything," she said to assuage Maggie's guilt, which betrayed itself in her expression.

"Please don't," said Maggie. "I don't want her to think she can't trust me."

Lee looked at her and twisted the gold ring on her finger. "I won't," she promised.

By now the boys were yelling down at them, telling them to hurry up, so they turned back to the sandy slide, conversation over.

9

After a few hours of playing on the dune, Julian eventually called it quits. The sun had reached its peak in the high noon sky, and scorched them mercilessly. Edward asked for more of their socks and made them into large, shady awnings to shelter them from the sun. They sat in easy silence with Eenie fast asleep on one of the rugs.

Lee sat up, half annoyed as she felt a familiar throb at her temples. With a resigned sigh, she closed her eyes and waited for the vision to pass.

> *A box was handed to Lee. She opened the lid.*
> *"Five-as-one, five-as-one, five-as-one, all-as-one . . ."*
> *the box echoed.*

Shaking her head, Lee waited for her vision to clear and looked around. The others hadn't seemed to notice, and Lee didn't think the vision was important enough to mention.

Julian passed her some fruit to snack on, and they talked in low voices so as not to wake Eenie.

"How are you doing?" Lee asked him, concerned by the tired lines around his eyes.

"Okay," he said, not quite meeting her eyes.

She wanted to ask him more but sensed he'd just evade her questions. Edward looked over, and an unspoken message passed between them.

"Let's set up the tent properly," Edward said, giving his brother a hand and hauling him to his feet. "I need your help to anchor it. It was far too windy last night!"

"True!" Julian agreed, with a bit of a grin. Edward cheerily teased Julian about something inconsequential. Lee watched her brothers with a tiny smile as they walked off, trading rude comments.

Nearby, Eenie yawned. Stretching like a small cat, she sat up and blearily looked around. "Can I have some?" she asked, rubbing her ears and looking at the fruit bowl.

"Isn't the desert huge?" Lee said, handing Eenie an apple. Eenie nodded, taking in the wide expanses of sand around them, and rubbed her ears again. Lee grabbed another apple for herself and took an enormous bite. "I think it's stunning though," she added, mouth full, gazing at the steep, powdered dunes.

"We're looking for a needle in a haystack," said Maggie, following her gaze.

"Or a grain of sand in a desert," Lee quipped.

Maggie groaned and rolled her eyes. Lee threw the apple at her, which she ducked easily.

Getting up to get more fruit, Lee noticed Eenie rubbing at her ears again. "What's wrong?"

"My ears keep ringing," Eenie said grumpily.

"It's probably just from the wind when we were in the bathtub," Lee said reassuringly.

Eenie grumbled something and rubbed hard at her ears again. "It feels like it's getting louder." She got up and walked to the edges of the camp, staring out to the horizon. Her blond hair glinted in the sun. She turned to her sisters, and pointed west. "I think it's coming from there."

"Really?" Lee said, coming over to stand next to her. She squinted but couldn't see anything.

"We should go over there," Eenie said in her little voice.

Looking down at her youngest sister, Lee pondered how young she really was and how they all seemed to forget that fact. *Still*, she thought, turning back to gaze in the westerly direction, *she's already proven herself more than capable.* Making up her mind, she told Maggie to get the boys.

"What's up?" asked Edward as he and Julian joined them.

"Eenie thinks we should go that way," Lee pointed. The boys followed her direction and gazed out at the never-ending expanse of sand. They turned back to her. Looking doubtful, Edward opened his mouth to say something but closed it when he saw Lee's expression. Julian just nodded when Lee turned to him with a raised eyebrow.

Lee and Eenie exchanged smiles as the boys packed up the camp. Although she'd got her way, Lee watched Julian with a small frown. Julian wouldn't have ever acquiesced that easily in the past. She watched him pack up with stilted movements. She was about to say something to him when—

"OUCH!"

Edward had smashed his elbow on something, and the next few minutes were spent furiously rubbing at his arm and swearing that a funny bone it most definitely was not. In the subsequent turmoil, the moment to speak to Julian passed.

"Do we fly there in the bathtub?" Maggie asked them. Edward shaded his eyes and looked out at the mountains of sand surrounding them.

"Hang on." He paused and wrinkled his nose as he squinted. "Is that a storm I see in the distance?" The others came to stand next to him. In a single horizontal line, the five looked out over the sandy ridges.

Lee studied the distant, light-coloured cloudy mass. "It doesn't look like rain."

Julian frowned. "There's definitely a cloud there though."

"Oh . . ." Edward groaned as the same thought hit them all at once.

"Sand storm!"

"It's definitely getting closer, too," Maggie cried, her voice rising.

They watched the darkening cloud approach their small camp. As it grew closer, they could make out the churning cloud in more detail as it whirled furiously towards them.

The sand whipped over the plains. Grains of sand raced each other in a frantic dash towards their campsite, tumbling and dancing madly as a tidal wave of yellow rushed furiously toward them.

Julian took a few steps towards the churning cloud, and stood there, eyes closed. A few tense moments later, he opened his eyes. "I can't stop it," he said, the line between his brows more pronounced than ever. "There's too much sand, and I can't move every grain!"

The wind soon picked up, whistling around them with a high keening noise. Their tent started to flutter, and the bowl of fruit suddenly tipped over, apples rolling away in all directions. Lee's eyes darted around the quaking campsite, trying to find something to help them.

Edward's nervousness was clear as he kept picking up objects, turning them into shields or armoured plates, then changing them back, muttering under his breath, "Not big enough . . . Not strong enough . . . That won't stop sand . . ."

Maggie was running after the apples, trying unsuccessfully to catch them. Chopsticks came out of the tent, took one look, and bolted in the opposite direction. Maggie called after the cat in dismay, her words lost in the whipping wind. Their tent was now flapping furiously, and with a sudden ripping noise, belted across the sand dunes, lost to sight in seconds.

"My sock!" exclaimed Maggie, watching it disappear.

Eenie's blue eyes darted around the camp as she watched her siblings' harried movements. She crouched down next to the bathtub to protect her skin from the flying sand.

"Let's try the five-as-one power!" Julian suddenly yelled at them. It immediately stopped them all in their tracks. With one synchronised movement, they circled around

Eenie and the bathtub. She stood up, looking tiny. The wind howled and whipped their hair into a frenzy as they held hands around her. They threw apprehensive glances at the approaching whirlwind.

Eenie stood facing Julian as he directed his siblings. They concentrated on Eenie as best they could, trying to ignore the sand whipping their faces and getting caught in their hair. The small girl raised her chin as they focused their attention.

Slowly, dully, a light glow encircled her small body.

"Keep at it," Julian muttered.

The storm frenzied as the glow grew brighter. The air around Eenie crackled as she faced Julian, eyes huge. The wind whipped through the circle while Julian yelled at them to keep concentrating and ignore the storm.

Sand dusted their skin and faces as the wind slapped against their bodies. Eenie glowed brighter, and her eyes turned from blue to a fiery white.

Lee flinched as the sand stung her face like a thousand needles. Julian's hand clenched hers even tighter. They were both white-knuckled as they concentrated harder on Eenie. The wind caused Lee's eyes to water as she watched Eenie glow with brilliant fire as the light from them surged forth in white-hot arrows.

The storm whirled around them in earnest as they lost sight of Eenie in the stinging sand. Julian yelled something, but his words were snatched away by the wind. The sand burned them with its stinging force. Lee couldn't see her siblings as they were swallowed by the storm. She felt Maggie and Julian's hands in hers and held on tightly.

The hands in hers suddenly went slack. The storm's harsh whistling became a muted screech. The white light from Eenie surrounded them as the sand that had been whipping them suddenly fell to the ground.

Lee's vision grew clearer as the sandy air dissipated. The whirling sand dervish still spun around their group, but it was now several feet away. It was as if they were in a soundproof bubble with a storm whirling and tapping on its outer edges.

Blinking furiously, they all looked at each and at their small sister in the middle, radiating light.

"Nice!" Edward exclaimed, looking around their little cocoon. Eenie's mouth twitched as she stood unnaturally still, her eyes still fiery white.

Maggie murmured, "I hope Chopsticks is okay," but no one really listened, intent on examining their soundproof bubble and casting Eenie half-worried, half-awed looks out of the corner of their eyes.

"How long will this hold?" Julian asked Eenie.

"Not long," she responded. Her voice was different—deeper and more adult than a five-year-old's.

Maggie spoke up. "I can find help, to get us to shelter."

"Quickly," Julian said with a glance at Eenie. She stood, silent and unmoving as her siblings tried to work out what to do next as quickly as they could. The storm raged on outside their bubble, beating against the invisible force with a constant pattering sound, like hail.

"What do we do with the bathtub?" Lee asked, looking at the tub, now filthy with sand clinging to its sides. Their bubble had encapsulated it as well.

"I'll bring it," Edward said. He touched the bathtub and changed it into a tiny version of itself. An impudent grin later and it had disappeared into his pocket.

"Here they are!" cried Maggie.

Out of the whirling storm lumbered five shaggy brown camels. They walked up to the bubble, and the invisible shield let them pass. Small gusts of sand ran in with the beasts, and the bubble pulsated until it was large enough to accommodate all of them.

The camels stood quietly, blinking at the suddenly still air and quietness. Outside, the sand rapped against the cocoon, the grains like tiny flies throwing themselves against a window.

"Look how beautiful they are!" Maggie affectionately stroked the long nose of the nearest camel. "They can help us through the sandstorm."

Julian and Lee came over cautiously to give them a pat. Edward stayed back, wrinkling his nose. "They stink!"

The camels had the strangest faces—side-placed eyes and long faces with rubbery lips. They were patient and stoic as the five crowded around them. Patting their dense, dirty fur, Lee studied their odd feet and faces with interest.

"They have three sets of eyelids and two rows of lashes to keep out the sand!" Maggie said, the admiration clear in her voice as she stroked one of their long necks.

"How do we get up?" Edward asked warily.

"Easy." Maggie said. She tossed her head back slightly. The camels bowed their long necks, and one by one, folded their front legs in front of them until they were sitting in the sand.

"Up we go!" Maggie said cheerfully. She picked up Eenie to place her on the first camel's back.

Eenie had been staring out at the sandstorm with eyes blazing, and barely seemed to notice what was happening around her. She was like a rag doll as Maggie and Julian sat her astride the shaggy brown animal. She held on automatically, grasping handfuls of its fur.

The other four climbed up carefully. After a few muted shrieks from the group as the camels rose to their full height, it wasn't long until they were all walking in a single file. Eenie and Maggie led the way, riding abreast. Their soundproof cocoon followed them as they moved through the desert. Lee marvelled at Eenie's power to hold the cocoon protectively around them, keeping the storm at bay.

A thought suddenly occurred to her.

"Can you use your powers while Eenie is absorbing them?" she asked Edward.

Julian overheard them.

"Don't do anything with your powers while Eenie is holding the sand!" he commanded. "It might cause the five-as-one link to break!"

Edward, for once, just nodded. They all looked around at their insular bubble with mesmerised expressions. It was pulsating slightly, like a balloon being squeezed, and was completely transparent, the storm outside a distant flurry.

The camels had a strange gait, and it took Lee a few moments to get used to it. The lolling, rolling walk dipped from side to side. *It's similar to a sway or twirl when dancing,* Lee mused. The camel she was on blew through its nose, and a gush of snot flew out.

Edward caught most of the spray on the back of his leg. "GROSS!" With a disgusted wipe against the camel's hairy sides, he threw a frown back at Lee as she fought furiously not to laugh.

They lumbered along in single file for some time. Eenie was as still as stone, sitting in total silence, eyes glowing with a bright white light as the bubble throbbed faintly around them.

"Whoa!" they all exclaimed as huge four-sided, triangular structures suddenly reared out from the sand before them. They were the same colour as the sand, and the group almost walked into the closest one before they saw them.

"They're so big! What are they?" Lee asked. She got no response. The others sat gazing up at the colossal structures, mouths hanging open. The four walls of each of the three structures rose up into the air to meet as a single point, and each structure was bigger than the last. The five gazed in silence at the trio of ancient architectural constructions, lost for words at the sheer size and power of them.

Eenie muttered under her breath, a sweat breaking out across her brow.

"Come on, let's get inside," Julian said, his brow creasing as he glanced at Eenie.

Maggie directed the camels over to the biggest structure. With hefty grunts, the camels bent their knees and crouched down in the sand. They waited patiently as the group clambered off their backs.

After a final pat, Maggie watched the camels nonchalantly walk back into the whirling sand, seeming not to notice the stinging storm.

"Here," Eenie motioned to the others, pointing out a small opening in one of the structures.

Eenie sighed softly as they entered. The sound of the whirling sandstorm was suddenly present again, and sand whipped across the entrance as they crouched in the small cavity.

"Great job, Eenie," Julian enthused, squeezing her shoulder. The others murmured the same. Eenie smiled up at them, looking exhausted.

"Let's rest here for a bit," Julian said, looking around at them. They were in some sort of tunnel, which gave enough cover to hold the whipping sand at bay. There was no argument from the others as they sprawled across the sandy floor, yawning, and fell asleep almost as soon they lay down.

10

Lee was startled awake. Looking around at the sleeping forms of her brothers and sisters, she wondered what had awoken her. Peering out the small opening of the tunnel, she realised the sandstorm had finally stopped. She woke up her siblings impatiently. She had had enough of lying on the hard ground and wanted to get going.

"Let me sleep," Edward groaned groggily.

"Come on, let's keep going and find a better place to set up camp," Lee said irritably. "This tunnel is hard and dark and small."

"Well, at least we're out of the sandstorm," Maggie said blearily, waking up with the others.

"It's stopped," Lee said. "Let's follow this tunnel into the structure and see where it goes."

They stumbled to their feet, and Edward made a small torchlight out of a stick in his pocket. The yellow beam showed them nothing but a black hole before them.

"Great," Edward muttered, his dislike of small spaces obvious.

Julian brought up the rear as they tentively walked through the narrow tunnel, single file. Lee led the way with the torch; Eenie and Maggie were next in line, then Edward, throwing the occasional comment over his shoulder to Julian. The dark, cramped confines threatened to overwhelm Lee at times, but she focused on the trembling yellow beam in front of her as she followed its light.

"Finally," Lee said as natural light appeared in the tunnel, a tiny slit at first, then a full beam of sunlight as they walked out into a cavern. Gazing around, Lee moved to one side of the tunnel exit as her siblings filed out behind her. She wandered off a bit as she took in her surroundings. The peaked ceiling seemed to go on for miles, and the ancient, crumbling stone around her was flaked and worn.

As Eenie came out of the tunnel, there was an excruciating screech.

"Sorry! Sorry!" Eenie pulled the madly wailing microphone from her pocket. Her fingers fumbled with it, and she turned it over, desperately looking for an off button. The others clapped their hands to their ears at the screeching, barely able to hear their own voices as they begged Eenie to turn it off. Eenie's hands trembled as she turned the deafening microphone over in her small hands, unable to find anything to stop the din.

"It's okay. Let me see," Maggie said, reaching to take it from Eenie. Eenie almost lost her hold on it, but Maggie caught it before it clattered to the ground. Maggie also had no luck, and the microphone continued to screech. Then, suddenly the microphone fell silent.

"There you go, Eenie!" Maggie said cheerfully, handing it back to her sister. The others rubbed their ears, grimacing.

Eenie took back the microphone with a tremulous smile and wiped her nose on her sleeve.

Lee noticed Eenie's self-consciousness at having four sets of eyes focused on her, and looked for something to divert their attention. She pointed at the wall behind them. "Check out those markings." The others turned to look at the strange shapes carved into it.

Edward walked over to it and stood with his hands on his hips, brow creasing. He traced one of the shapes with his fingers. "It's . . . Look!" His finger had traced the shape of a horse.

Julian came closer and peered at it. "It has a horn," he said quietly, pointing to the stumpy protrusion from the animal's forehead.

The five stood quietly, staring at the carving and the rows upon rows of figures carved into the stone.

"This is the next clue," Julian stated.

"Maggie, look at this one," Lee said, pointing to another figure. A long spindly bird appeared several times in the rows of markings.

"My ibis," Maggie said in a hushed voice.

"It reads like a story or a sentence, I think," Lee mused, following the row with her eyes. She pointed at a figure with an ibis head and a man's body partially covered by a loincloth. He held a spear in one hand. "See, the bird becomes half-man, half-bird in this next row."

"What's that next to him?" Maggie asked, peering at the crumbling wall.

"Looks like the moon," Julian said quietly. Lee stared at the crescent shape, thinking about their blue-moon gateway.

"That looks like a sundial as well," said Edward. "Maybe it means time?"

"Ibis-man, moon, time and . . . writing?" Julian guessed, pointing at a scroll carving, the next image in the picture-sentence.

"Look at this one," Maggie traced the outline. A woman's curvy shape was etched into the sandstone, wings on her back, above a crowd of people. A lone man stood apart from the crowd, staring up at her.

"This one," Lee said, pointing to a peaked carving. "It must mean a mountain?"

"Too many coincidences," Edward remarked. "Surely this is telling us to go to the mountains next?"

"Oh my gosh!" Maggie gasped, drawing their attention to the next row of carvings, where five crudely drawn stick figures were depicted.

"That settles it." Julian paused and stared again at the figures, his brow creasing. "But . . . how can that be? Aren't these structures thousands of years old?"

"The Professor might have drawn them," Edward said, not sounding convinced.

They stared up at the wall, then around them at the tri-angular structure. Carvings covered every single inch of it.

"He might have . . . " Edward's voice trailed off.

A tentative miaow sounded nearby. Chopsticks sauntered into the cavern, her tail held high, looking like she didn't have a care in the world. Maggie picked her up with a cry of delight, and stroked her until she was purring, eyes blissfully closed. She eventually placed the cat on the floor, joining the others to muse over the carvings. Eenie sat cross-legged on the ground with Chopsticks, playing with the microphone, while the others talked in low voices, trying to work out what the strange markings meant.

A static crackling noise sounded out around them that gradually turned into a voice. ". . . careful . . ."

The five looked at each other with varying expressions of confusion.

". . . not a friend . . .!" The voice faded in and out. Lee's arms suddenly broke out in goosebumps. The voice sounded familiar to her although she couldn't place it.

". . .careful . . ."

". . . not a friend . . ."

". . .careful . . ."

The garbled static noise echoed all around them. The cavernous space and high-pointed ceiling made the words sound like they were coming right out of the walls. The voice and static faded away, until there was nothing but silence.

Maggie crouched down next to Eenie, and they held hands tightly. Lee frowned as she pondered the words. Julian's brow was deeply creased. Edward tried to look scornful but failed miserably.

"What . . .what was that?" Maggie's voice broke slightly as she spoke.

"It was strange that happened while we were here," Lee said with a feeling of increasing dread.

"Was it a warning?" Julian said, frowning up at the cavernous ceiling. "About who though?"

"It probably means nothing," said Edward. They convinced themselves it was just a strange fluke.

They left the cavern immediately, still not sure what had happened. Their instincts clearly told them it was time to go, so back down the tunnel they headed, and out into the sandy desert.

* * *

The five tried to make sense of what the voice had told them. After going round in circles for over half an hour, Julian eventually held up his hand. "Enough." He sounded more like his old self than he had for a while. "There's no point going over it again. Someone could just have been playing a cruel prank."

Edward opened his mouth to speak, but closed it after Julian glared at him, gesturing slightly towards Eenie. Her eyes had been glimmering ever since they'd left the structures, and her face was bright red.

Edward nodded once and changed the subject. "I did see mountains as we were flying," he said to his brother. Julian looked slightly relieved. The boys stood there for a moment, discussing their next move. The girls stood silently, sand dusting over their shoes lightly as they stood staring out at the yellow expanse.

Chopsticks suddenly hissed and spat, her tiny back arched. Her tail pointed straight up as she stared at a sand dune in the distance, her eyes dilated.

"What is it?" Maggie asked, frowning slightly. The cat hissed again and then suddenly bolted.

"Chopsticks!" Maggie called, her arms stretched out in front of her as the small creature ran back towards the structures, soon lost to sight.

"Maggie, look!" Edward grabbed her arm, pulling her back from chasing after the cat. Two sets of pricked ears appeared suddenly, like tiny triangles over the sand dunes.

The five watched, three giant structures forming a backdrop, as a sandy-haired head with black spots peeked over the dune. A second sandy head appeared after it. Soon, sinuous and graceful, two large cheetahs padded over the sandy ground towards them.

The cheetahs were slim and rangy with deep chests and lanky legs. Their tails were long, and their fur was a tawny colour with solid black spots dotted evenly over their bodies. Maggie told her siblings the dots on their skins were like their names; each had unique markings.

As the cheetahs walked gracefully towards them, the five could see a small girl riding on the back of the first animal, and an even smaller girl on the back of the second. As they swayed side to side on the backs of the cats, the two girls waved at the group. The cheetahs stopped near their gathering, and the girls slid off their backs in one lithe movement. They walked with soft bare feet on the sand, moving elegantly towards the Delliks.

Lee had been watching the taller girl closely. She seemed familiar. Her eyes were warm, amber brown and the curls that sprung from her head jet-black. She smiled at Lee. This jogged Lee's memory, and she grinned back in delight.

It was the child she'd met in the floating world. The one she'd given the Box-with-no-Bottom to.

Aequalis was the world's name, Lee thought to herself, remembering Mr Lennon's words. She couldn't stop grinning, and when the girl drew near, Lee blurted out an excited, "You're from Aequalis?"

Her siblings exclaimed softly at the memory of the strange floating land.

The girl's curls bounced slightly as she nodded, her dark honey eyes staring back at the rest of group.

"My name is Zoya. It was meant to be that we would meet again here," she said, her mouth curling upwards into a lovely smile, showing bright white teeth against her dark skin. Lee and Zoya gave each other a tentative hug, strangers in one sense, but so much more than that. Zoya gestured to her left. "This is my twin sister Zara."

The smaller girl smiled shyly and nodded slightly, but remained silent.

Zoya talked animatedly. "When you defeated Mediarn, we had no reason to stay in Aequalis. We followed our spirituality and were drawn to this place." She gestured sweepingly at the structures.

"Spirituality?" Lee said in curiosity.

"Spirituality is just another term for awareness," Zoya said. "Such awareness was lacking during Mediarn's rule."

Eenie's eyes narrowed slightly at the mention of her captor.

Zoya gestured at the grand triangular constructs around them. "We were drawn to this place." She paused and sighed. "But it's not like it once was. These used to be a key part of creating awareness in this world. Now they just crumble as forgotten relics."

Edward shrugged, losing interest. "Where are your parents?" he asked, impatiently digging his toes into the sand.

"They died," Zoya replied monotonically, staring blankly at the structures.

"Oh." Edward's face reddened.

"They were killed in Aequalis." Zara bent her head at her sister's words.

"Killed?" Maggie said, her eyes softening while her lips curled in a grimace.

Zara nodded. "By Mediarn."

Lee remembered all too well what the other people in that world had been like. "I'll bet you had no one to help you either," she said almost to herself, her voice hard.

Zoya gave a half-smile. "We learnt to survive by ourselves." Her face suddenly transformed into a full smile, directed wholly at Lee. "With some help from a kind and generous stranger." Lee went pink as Zoya stared at her with shining eyes.

"Come," Zoya gestured to them. "I have something to give you."

They watched as she walked over to one of the cheetahs and took down a large saddlebag.

"Riding those must be amazing," Edward said, appraising the animals with an impressed look.

"They are the fastest animals on land," Zoya said, the pride in her voice unmistakable. "They are also extremely loyal, and do not take to strangers."

This was evidently a warning aimed at Edward, who had stretched his hand out towards the nearest cheetah. He snatched it back as the cheetah bared its short white teeth. Zoya and Maggie laughed at his expression.

Zara had been rummaging through the saddle bag, and bowed her head as she handed something to her sister. It was a small wooden box.

"The Box-with-no-Bottom!" the four older Delliks cried in unison, while Eenie stared at it curiously.

Zoya handed it reverently to Lee. "It has helped us immeasurably. It's now time to return it to you."

Lee carefully took the box from Zoya's hands. Looking down at the square chest, she noticed thin slivers of crystal quartz running subtly through the wood.

Zoya spoke. "Remember, it will give you whatever you need at the time you open it. You gifted us the Box in Aequalis, so that is where you will have full use of its power."

The five stared at each other. Lee's fingers tightened on the box. Edward's mouth fell open as he looked at it intently. Eenie put her hands on Lee's arm to peer up at it more closely. Maggie and Julian's shoulders knocked together as they stared enraptured.

Maggie whispered what they were all thinking. "The Professor!"

Lee grinned at the four of them. "Surely the Box could tell us where he is?"

Julian's brow creased in its familiar way. "We have to go back to Aequalis though?" He sounded troubled.

"Is there any other way of getting there, apart from the Professor's house?" Maggie asked Zoya. "We're so far from there."

"I don't know. I'm sorry," said Zoya. "We came here through the dark worlds."

Zara spoke up for the first time, her voice a gentle whisper. "If you head to the mountains, there is someone who may be able to help you."

"Oh!" The five looked at each other in suppressed excitement, remembering the mountains they'd seen depicted earlier.

"All signs lead to the mountains," Lee announced, looking to Julian, who nodded in agreement.

Thinking of the ancient symbols they'd seen, Lee asked Zoya, "Do you know anything about bicorns?"

Zoya, who was now brushing one of the cheetahs with a thick-bristled brush, stopped dead in her tracks. Zara whispered something darkly to herself and made a curious gesture over her chest, like a ward or prayer.

"How do you know about bicorns?" Zoya asked, her voice suddenly tense and almost angry. Edward shot Julian a look and opened his mouth to explain, but Lee spoke first. "They only appear when there is evil afoot in world."

"The last time was when Mediarn came to power," Zara whispered.

"The Professor told us about them," she said quickly, shooting Edward a warning look.

Zoya's shoulders relaxed slightly, but her mouth was a hard, thin line. "Bicorns come from Aequalis," she explained, nodding gravely at their stunned expressions. "They ravaged our cities constantly. There are dark stories that follow them, wherever they go."

Zara kept murmuring to herself whilst making the curious gestures in front of her chest.

"There were rumours that some unicorns had gone mad," Zoya said grimly. "Some said they were somehow connected to the bicorns . . ." Her voice trailed off as she stared unseeingly into the distance.

A small noise issued deep from within Maggie's throat. The others were silent, remembering their magical ride on the unicorns.

"A human and a unicorn often bond with each other," Zoya explained. "It's a bond for life and a symbiotic one for the human and the unicorn."

"They're mentally intertwined and become physically dependent on each other," Zara interjected softly at their confused faces.

"If the rumours are true that some of the unicorns had gone mad," Zoya's eyes turned distant. "Well . . . it may have been to do with their bond with their humans . . ."

"Not all humans have the best intentions," Zara growled.

Lee blinked at the venom in her voice.

"Nothing can stop or destroy bicorns," Zoya said, refocusing her eyes on the five. "It's best not to speak of them at all."

Julian stared at Edward with an almost imperceptible shake of his head, and the subject was dropped.

‖

"It's getting late," Zoya said. "You should stay here for the night and travel again tomorrow. You are welcome to come stay in our camp."

The five were relieved and accepted the offer without hesitation.

"We don't camp in the desert," Zoya explained. "There is more shelter on the savannah. It lies over that way, on the edges of the desert." She stretched out her arm, pointing into the far distance. "Come, you will travel with us on the cheetahs." She gestured towards the sleek animals stretched out on the sandy ground. "They will get us there quickly."

Edward blinked a few times. Zoya laughed at his expression. "Never fear, they are more docile than they look." Edward didn't look convinced but followed the others as they walked towards the supple creatures.

"I think I'll walk," he said quickly as the girls patted the fur of the elegant animals. They smiled knowingly when Julian said he'd do the same, to keep his brother company.

Eenie, Maggie and Zara rode astride the back of one cheetah, with Zoya and Lee on the other. Lee stroked the fur beneath her in wonder; the black spots were much softer to touch than the dense yellow fur beneath it. She marvelled when Zoya told her the cheetahs' paws had hard pads, a bit like rubber, that allowed them to walk comfortably on the hot sand.

The boys trailed along a few metres behind so the sand tossed up from the cheetah's feet didn't shower them. Edward spoke for most of the way until he realised he was getting nothing but monosyllabic answers from his brother. He gave Julian a bit of a push.

"What's up?" he asked playfully.

Julian glanced sideways at Edward. "Nothing," he said curtly.

"What do you mean, 'nothing'? You've barely spoken all day. And you haven't even told me off lately for using my powers in public." Edward waggled his eyebrows.

Julian shrugged.

Edward's cheeky expression faded as he looked at his brother more closely. "Seriously, Julian, what's the matter?"

Julian raised one shoulder in a half-shrug and still said nothing. Edward got an obstinate look on his face and opened his mouth to say more when Julian said in a low voice, "I can't stop thinking about it."

"Thinking about what?"

"The Professor dying . . . " Julian trailed off.

Edward first retort died on his lips as he looked at his brother's downcast expression. He sighed. "You're not to blame."

"I should have stopped it," Julian muttered. "I should have done more."

"Mediarn was too powerful," Edward said quietly. "We could only defeat him when we were all together."

Julian shook his head, shoulders slumped.

"You can't keep blaming yourself," Edward stated. "Besides, the Professor might still be alive."

"That's not for certain," Julian said. "This could be a wild goose chase for all we know."

Edward watched his brother, uncertain how to respond. He wasn't used to Julian being so down and defeatist; he'd always been their anchor in times of uncertainty.

"It'll be okay," he finally said.

Julian stayed silent for the rest of the walk, with Edward's attempts at cheerful conversation falling on deaf ears.

* * *

Their surroundings slowly but surely changed from peaked sandy dunes to flatter, lighter ground. The sand cleared, with small, scrubby bushes now dotting the landscape.

The twins' camp was simple but comfortable, set in a small glade of stunted trees. Its makeshift walls were rough pieces of wood lashed together by ropes and covered with blankets. On the floor were numerous tightly woven mats, sprinkled with sand but still comfortable. The five took off their shoes with sighs of relief, glad to be barefoot like their hostesses. Small trinkets adorned rough ledges built into the wooden beams, and hand-drawn pictures decorated the walls, giving the place a homely and cosy feel.

"Let me help you," Maggie said to Zara as she started pulling out old, dented metal pans and filling them with water from a nearby bucket.

Julian volunteered to get wood for the fire from a roughly made storage shack a few metres away. Lee sensed he wanted to be alone, and shook her head at Edward's enquiring glance. They both watched him walk along the savannah, shoulders slumped.

"I really hope we find the Professor." Edward's muted words echoed both of their thoughts.

Ecnie lay on one of the mats, too tired to do much else. Maggie and Zara busied themselves with getting dinner ready, as Zoya poured sweet tea into chipped golden-metal cups, which she passed around to them. Lee took a sip. The tea tasted of cloves and honey, and she didn't say no when it was offered a second and third time.

Zara was the quieter of the two sisters, and mostly watched Zoya with a soft smile, not speaking unless spoken to. Maggie tried to draw her out in conversation by asking about the triangular structures.

"They have been here for millennia," Zara said in her soft voice. "They are some of the oldest structures in this world, and they hold many secrets." Her liquid brown eyes shone as she talked. She told Maggie, now spellbound, that they had been built off the backs of slaves. They were monuments to kings gone by. "They have mysteries that are hidden to this day." Zara's voice was mesmerising, and Maggie was enthralled by her words as she watched the sinking sun cast a low glow against her dark skin. Zara's eyes shone with a beautiful depth in the twilight.

Yellow rays turned to dull red then dark amber as the dying sun settled below the horizon. The sandy dunes in the distance, once a cheerful yellow, were now a moody dark brown, and their peaks looked more pronounced.

The Delliks didn't have much to contribute to the meal, as their supplies had almost entirely gone. Edward used his powers to make the last of their bread rolls grow to enormous sizes. Zara pan-fried the bread in some oil until it was crunchy and delicious. Zoya brought out some dried leaves, dried fruit, and some hard nuts to share.

Julian had brought back an armful of wood, and they had a crackling fire to keep them warm as the evening cooled. They were all silent for the most part, worn out from the day. The only sounds to be heard were the popping of wood in the fire, the loud crunching of hard nuts between teeth, and a murmured word here and there.

"Oh!" In an instant Maggie sat up straighter and peered out of the camp. With a sudden gasp, she grabbed Lee's arm. "There are elephants nearby!" she exclaimed, delight clear in her voice. A loud trumpeting punctuated her words.

The group turned towards the noise. The elephants trumpeted, closer this time, and the heavy thud of footsteps caught their ears. Two enormous grey elephants soon appeared before the entrance to the camp, walking in a stately way on their huge tree-trunk legs. The five marvelled at the saggy skin that covered their bodies, and the massive ears that flapped cheerfully as their small, black eyes twinkled at the group. Trunks raised, the elephants drew near as the five, along with Zara and Zoya, stood up and walked out of the camp to meet them.

"There's no way I'm riding that!" Edward exclaimed, staring up at the huge beasts.

"They wouldn't let you anyway," Maggie said loftily. One of elephant's trunks curled like a grey arm around her shoulder. She giggled as it rubbed against her neck. Her eyes grew unfocused.

"They are majestic creatures," Zoya said, stroking one of the trunks that had wrapped around her shoulders in familiarity. "They talk to each other through their feet and feel each other's vibrations through the ground."

"Vibrations," Lee murmured as she watched Zoya smile up at the creature who had embraced her.

The moon shone brightly in the clear night sky, illuminating the scene before them. Tiny stars blinked into view, like fireflies caught in a huge web. The group stared up into the sky, watching the twinkling lights burst out in a feverish light show.

The savannah grew chillier as darkness crept up on them. They wrapped themselves snugly in tightly woven blankets. These were a luxury after being whipped with sand and sleeping on the hard, sand-packed floor of the tunnel, and it wasn't long until they nodded off around the campfire. The elephants stayed close to the camp as the group slept.

* * *

They were woken from their sleep by a loud scream that tore through the night air.

"Eenie! Eenie!" Maggie had awoken instantly and was calling her name.

Eenie was sobbing, her cheeks wet with tears.

"What is it?" Lee was by her side in a flash, following Maggie by only a moment.

Zoya and Zara sat up and blearily peered over.

"It's fine, go back to sleep." Maggie waved at them to lie back down, which they did, while still keeping their eyes on the girls.

"What is it?" Edward and Julian were now right there beside them too.

"She's had a nightmare," Maggie whispered back. "It's okay." Maggie took Eenie in her arms and rocked her gently, saying in a soothing voice, "It's okay, it's okay."

Eenie hiccupped once or twice and gradually quietened. Her eyelids drooped as Maggie rocked her in her arms. Edward made to speak, but Maggie shook her head at him. He stayed quiet until Eenie fell asleep. Julian gently plucked her from Maggie's arms and carried her back to her bed.

Returning to the others, he quietly said, "Poor Eenie. She's been through so much and has been such a trooper through everything since."

"We forget how young she is," Maggie agreed.

"After this, we'll need to try and make life as normal as possible for her," said Julian. Edward's lips twitched at this. Julian looked sheepish as he realised what he'd said. "Well, you know," he amended. "As normal as it gets for us."

The four sat in silence, watching the last of the fire spit and pop, and one by one they fell back asleep as the embers grew dim.

* * *

The next morning, the twins told them there was a watering hole nearby they could swim in before breakfast.

"Let's go for a walk and take a look," Maggie said to Lee and Eenie. They nodded, and the boys called to them as they headed off. "Be careful! We'll follow you in a bit."

Walking along the savannah, the girls pointed out the exotic and strange-looking animals they passed. Tall, gangly-legged giraffes, necks stretching up to the furthest corners of the trees to tear off leaves. Wide, big-bellied buffalo with curved, dangerous-looking horns. Small antelope leapt past them, their small, lean bodies covered in yellow spots on short brown hair.

Maggie's eyes were unfocused as she spoke to a lion far away. She told the girls, much to their disappointment, that he didn't like humans and wouldn't come any closer.

Eventually Maggie cried, "Look!" She pointed towards the horizon, where a large glimmer winked on and off. It shone more as the girls drew closer.

"It looks like a star!" Eenie said with childlike delight.

"I think it's water," Maggie grinned.

They walked towards the glimmer. The image started to sharpen at the edges until they could make out the edges of a gently rippling lake.

At first it seemed like it wasn't far away, but by the time they reached the edge of the lake they were all puffing and panting from a good twenty minutes of walking.

Maggie echoed their thoughts. "It's beautiful."

The blue oasis was nirvana in the middle of the hot and dusty savannah. Long, cool ripples of water lapped lazily on the bank, like cotton sheets tossed in the breeze. The blue water was in stark contrast to the sparse, yellow savannah. Yellow light glinted on the wet surface, and the water looked like azure silk glimmering with tiny sparks of gold. Fine droplets blew across their faces, a relief from the constant spray of sand.

"There are fish in there!" Maggie cried, surprised. "They're very young, and they don't live for very long, but they love it here." She crouched down by the water's edge, her attention caught by the lake's inhabitants.

Lee soon grew bored watching Maggie converse silently with the fish, and wandered off around the shoreline with Eenie trailing along behind. The girls gazed out at the water and watched as a huge bubble broke on the surface. Eenie thought it was wonderful and giggled as other bubbles popped in quick succession.

The bubbles came faster, and the girls watched in awe

as a large hippo raised his head languidly out of the water and gazed at them with small, beady eyes. With a yawn, he showed them his huge mouth, with its pink, slimy tongue and white, pegged teeth, before closing his powerful jaws again with a snap. Three more bald heads poked out of the water, blinking at the girls.

Eenie squealed. "I love them! I'll call that one Minty, that one Milo, that one Cherry, and that one Sasha!" She reeled off the names as she pointed to each of the animals in turn.

Maggie caught up to them, giggling as she told Eenie they were actually very serious animals, and they didn't much like their names. Eenie pointed her chin upwards and declared to the hippos that their names were pretty and they should like them.

Lee was just as much in thrall as her sisters as the shiny, grey beasts rolled over in the water and showed off for them.

"Julian still seems to be in a funk," Maggie said suddenly. She lowered her voice so Eenie wouldn't overhear them as she stood pointing at the hippos, loudly declaring their names once more.

"I know," Lee muttered without turning her head. "He hasn't been the same since the Professor died."

"But he's alive! Mr Lennon said he was!" Maggie's voice strained with desperation.

Lee shrugged. "The best we can do is try. Although Julian doesn't seem to even want to do that."

"Well, it's up to us to convince him it's worth it." Maggie turned to her sister, her lips firm. Lee looked at her and wondered when she'd grown up so suddenly.

"You're right."

Their conversation stopped as they noticed Julian and Edward had caught up and were walking towards them. Lee flopped down on a grassy patch by the muddy bank and stretched out her legs. She watched lazily as Edward tried to tempt the girls into the water with him. Julian sprawled on the grass next to Lee, not saying much. Lee gave up trying to make a conversation with him, content to watch the others in silence.

Maggie eventually gave in to Edward's persuading but soon regretted it after she was dunked by him immediately after getting in. She came up spluttering, spitting out a mouthful of water, and crossly pushed him away.

"Too much!" Maggie got out of the water in a huff. Her mood quickly turned when Chopsticks made a reappearance at the water's edge, having managed somehow to track them down. Maggie was thrilled, the others less so, with Edward muttering something that sounded suspiciously like, "Annoying little thing . . . Keeps turning up . . ."

Maggie resolutely placed the cat on her shoulders as they walked back to camp.

Soon, they bade farewell to the twins, with effusive thanks all round for the Box and their hospitality. Edward pulled the tiny transformed bathtub out of his pocket and used his powers to change it back. It wasn't long until they were waving exuberantly to their new friends as the bathtub rose swiftly. Shooting through the air like an arrow, they headed towards their next destination—the mountains.

12

Maggie's ibises gathered around the bathtub, croaking throatily as the wind whistled in their ears. The bathtub sliced straight and fast through the air. It started to feel a lot cooler as they left behind the savannah plains and flew towards distant rocky peaks.

After a time, they started descending. Lee exclaimed, "Watch out Julian!" as the bathtub almost bumped into a mountain peak emerging from the thinning clouds.

He gave a grunt and frowned as the bathtub wobbled. It floated down a little more gently after that.

The mountains soon surrounded them. Vast and rocky, they stretched for miles. The peaks looked like chocolate swirls; whorls and curls were patterned into the rock. Craggy slopes encircled them, and Julian had to concentrate very carefully to navigate through the giant outcrops.

Finally, they landed gently on a stony alcove, nestled within the steep, stony slopes. They piled out of the bathtub and glanced around them. The bathtub looked very odd amongst the dark boulders of the mountain. Lee stared in awe at the towering rocky ranges, feeling very small and insignificant.

"We must be very high up," she said softly. Somehow

she felt speaking in a low tone was more appropriate with the rocky wonder around her.

Edward was gazing in the opposite direction. "Someone's coming," he told his siblings over his shoulder. Slowly but surely, a man appeared, walking in a relaxed and stately manner towards them.

"Who else could be this high up in the mountains?" Maggie mused. Chopsticks gave a familiar low growl and bolted off again.

"That cat is just plain irritating," Edward said as Maggie looked downcast again, watching the tiny creature bound gracefully over the rocky stone and disappear from sight. She turned her back to her brother.

The five waited in silence as the figure approached them. His gait seemed somewhat familiar.

"Haven't we met him before?" Edward said to Julian in a low undertone.

Julian narrowed his eyes, looking faintly shocked. "It's the chief from one of the worlds!"

"Consecutio!" Maggie exclaimed. "The world was called Consecutio."

"He was from that tribe," Lee agreed. "I thought they had orange skin."

"I'm sure it's him!" said Edward.

The man approaching didn't have orange skin, but he was wearing a bright orange robe slung over one shoulder. He had a shaven head, and his brown, almond-shaped eyes creased in the corners as he smiled at them and gave a low bow. "We meet again," he said, throwing a quick wink in Edward's direction.

"We met you in Consecutio, didn't we?" Lee asked.

"Yes, you did," he said with a small, sharp nod. "Everyone moved on after you liberated us from the evil magic. I am known as the Elder here. I knew of your coming through the music. The five rhythms." He smiled affectionately at the five. "Come. I will take you to my dwelling."

The high mountain paths were treacherous, and the five progressed very slowly. Maggie held Eenie's hand after the little girl fell over while walking along the rocky ground.

"Follow me in single file; it will be the safest way," the Elder said smoothly.

Julian was last in line, and concentrated both on walking and conducting the porcelain bathtub to bob along in their wake. Maggie and Eenie stayed close to each other in the middle of the line, and Lee and Edward questioned the Elder as they proceeded.

"Why is your skin brown now, when it was orange when we first met?" Lee queried.

"Nothing but paint, child." The Elder smiled indulgently. "The tradition of this tribe is that we wear tunics and cowls."

He pointed up to the mountain with the highest peak. "You are blessed to be in the shadow of Chomolungma. She is the Goddess."

"Where are you taking us exactly?" Edward asked as they trudged uphill. It was tough going. Lee's knees started aching as they scaled the rocks. Julian told them to slow down as Maggie and Eenie fell further and further behind. Finally, Julian picked up Eenie and placed her in the bathtub. With a small exclamation, she gripped the sides in delight as Julian kept it afloat.

They continued to climb, Eenie in the bathtub, grinning widely at them all. Edward made a smart comment about joining Eenie, but was told it took more effort with more of them in it and to keep walking. Slipping and sliding on the loose stones, the four were soon wheezing in the brisk air.

"It's the altitude, dears," said the Elder sympathetically as their breathing became laboured. "Here, try chewing on this leaf. It will help you."

He handed them all short, fat green leaves. They munched on them, and gradually felt their heads clear and their fatigue start to fade. It was much easier after that.

* * *

After half an hour of walking, the Elder drew them to a rocky outcrop and gestured outwards.

Puffing, the group slowly caught up, one by one, and stood next to him to look out at the startling view. An encampment filled the horizon as far as the eye could see. Tents and rustic stone campsites were scattered across it, with brightly coloured flags strung between them, gaily flapping in the wind. The campsites hugged the mountain ranges around them, nestled into the base of the rocks.

"Oh," Eenie said softly. She pointed. There, at the far reaches of the encampment, was an astounding temple. It had hundreds and hundreds of steps and reached towards the sky. Painted in white, dark red, and yellow, it looked formidable and magnificent.

"That's where reverence and respect is paid," said the Elder, following their gaze. "Its an ancient structure, over 1400 years old in this world."

This world? Lee thought.

"Come, we are going to a different place." The Elder gestured in the opposite direction to much more modest-looking dwellings. As they followed him downwards towards the encampment, bronzed men passed them, carrying large sticks across the backs of their shoulders. Lashed to each end was an enormous canvas bundle, tied up with rope.

"Aren't they heavy?" Lee asked the Elder as they passed another man, sweating under the weight of the bundles.

"Extremely heavy." The Elder nodded at Eenie. "Probably the weight of this young one, twice over."

"Why are they carrying so much then?" Edward asked.

"It is a necessity for their livelihood," the Elder replied.

Lee noticed the men wore braided thongs of leather on their feet, and no shoes at all. She marvelled at their endurance.

Arriving at the fringes of the camp, they came to a brightly coloured stone structure with a blanket hanging as a door.

"Wait here a moment, dears." The Elder moved the blanket and ducked inside.

Maggie groaned. Lee followed her gaze to where several yaks were tethered. They were sturdy and short, much smaller than horses, with coarse auburn hair sprouting from their foreheads like a fringe. "They're miserable," said Maggie. "The people here are going to eat them."

Edward gave her a friendly nudge, and the ropes that tethered the yaks suddenly turned into daisy-chains.

Maggie giggled as the yaks slowly realised what had happened, then started lumbering away. She beamed at Edward.

The Elder gestured to them. "In here, dears."

The five filed in.

The interior was filled with colourful objects. Bright pink blankets, vivid blue shawls, and striking green swatches of material hung from the walls. Copper saucepans, kettles, and pans swung from the roof. In the middle of the room was a large wooden crate, and on top of it were shiny metal teacups with a steaming kettle next to them. A man crouching beside the box bowed his shaved head. He wore robes like the Elder's, but they were dark red rather than orange.

"This is my apprentice," the Elder said by way of introduction. The five nodded back to him.

Maggie did a double take and gaped at him. "Vita!"

"We meet again," the small man bowed to Maggie, much lower this time.

The five were thrilled and chatted with him, remembering

their time with him at the Dome in the blue world - Partior. They learnt he had left the Dome to come and work with the Elder in the mountains. He was much more pleasant than at their last meeting, but spoke mostly just to Maggie.

Vita explained he'd left the worlds behind, like many others, once Mediarn had been vanquished. While his brethren had been drawn to different places, he had been drawn to the mountains.

"There's a rumour afoot," he said in a low voice to Maggie.

She raised her eyebrows and drew closer to him. "About what?" She copied his low tone.

"There's rumours in Partior," he paused and waited until Edward, who had shifted closer, moved away again. "They say . . . he said in a lower tone. Maggie was now almost on top of him trying to listen. ". . . that one of Mediarn's sons survived."

"Whaaaat," Maggie's word came out strangled.

He shook his head at her quickly and gestured furiously at her gasp. Maggie tried immediately to draw him out with more questions, but Vita excused himself politely after a while.

Reappearing moments later, he placed several dishes on the table. On small, dusty gold plates he served a stew with dates, figs and walnuts, giving Maggie the biggest serving. He poured them steaming tea out of a shiny silver teapot with interesting engravings on it.

Vita placed a few tins on the table, then after another

deferential bow made his way out of the room. Lee watched him as he passed a wilted potted flower near the back doorway. Vita touched it lovingly, crooning a few soft words before leaving the room.

"What are these?" Edward asked with a mouthful of stew, picking up one of the tins.

"Oh, that's canned air," said the Elder.

Edward almost spat out his stew. "Canned air?" His voice was garbled as he tried to swallow.

The Elder smiled and handed him a napkin. "Yes, the locals swear by it. They go up to the northernmost tips of the mountain and collect the air."

The group looked at each other with raised eyebrows, mouths open disbelievingly.

The Elder waved his hand, dismissing it. "It's really just a gimmick they sell to tourists. Funnily enough, it's one of their biggest sellers."

Focused on the Elder, the others didn't notice when Lee's eyes rolled into the back of her head and she briefly blacked out.

"Connected . . . connected . . . consequence . . . consciousness . . ."

Blinking hard, Lee came back to the sounds of her siblings' chattering and laughter. *Vague as usual*, Lee thought, irritated. She rubbed her finger where the gold ring had been burning. Shrugging to herself, she picked up her fallen fork and kept eating.

The five continued to eat with relish, realising they were starving. Soon, their chatter grew loud and a bit rowdy.

"You'll wake the dragon with that racket," said the Elder. "He lives on this mountain."

The five looked at him with various expressions of surprise and apprehension, and sheer scepticism from Edward.

"Never fear," said the Elder with a short laugh. "The dragon is a tale that the older folk tell the children to scare them into being good."

The five laughed and the meal continued.

At last they sat back, bellies full, feeling content.

The Elder withdrew something from his robe. "Edward, this belongs to you."

"My pocket watch!" Edward looked delighted as the Elder passed over a long golden chain with the small, intricately cased clock dangling at its end.

"I believe it only works in Consecutio, but you may want it for sentimental value," the Elder said.

Edward held the pocket watch carefully. "Yes, it belonged to my parents." His fingers tightened. "I thought I'd left it there. Thank you for bringing it back!"

The Elder nodded, looking pleased.

The long benches they had sat on around the table turned into beds for the night with the help of a few comfortable blankets. Soon, the lights went out, and they fell fast asleep.

13

The next morning, Julian and Edward rose first, with Lee and Eenie grudgingly waking soon after.

"Maggie, breakfast is ready." Edward plonked a plate down next to his sister's bed. He kept chattering at her, expecting her to rise at any moment.

"Who are you talking to?" Maggie called from the doorway.

The group laughed heartily as they realised Edward had been speaking to a pile of blankets.

Julian picked up Lee's backpack, which had fallen over in the night. He scooped up the items that had tumbled out and started to repack them. The Elder came into the room just as he was about to put the book back in the bag.

"The Skilled Book!" The Elder gazed at it with wonder and awe.

"You know it?" Edward asked with interest.

The Elder was looking at the book with an expression close to worship. "That book is an ancient and hallowed manuscript going back generations." He fell to his knees and bowed his head to Julian. Julian held the book awkwardly and looked at the others for help. Lee and Maggie smiled into their palms.

The Elder put his hands to his forehead and continued. "It has been told that no one can read it apart from a Delliks, and if anyone tries, they go blind." He touched his forehead to the floor.

Lee watched her brother become more and more uncomfortable as the Elder started to chant in a low voice. Edward grinned widely.

Eenie stared with a curious expression at the prostrated man. "What were you singing?" she asked when he stopped.

"I wasn't singing, child. I was chanting." He smiled at the little girl. "It's called a mantra."

"What does that mean?" Eenie said, eyes bright.

"A mantra means saying the same thing over and over again," said the Elder.

"Why would you want to do that?" Eenie asked, blinking.

"We do it to give respect, or to reinforce positive things."

"Oh." Eenie mulled over that. She smiled up at him innocently. "Can it be used to reinforce bad things then?"

The Elder frowned slightly. "Well, I suppose so, but that's not its intent." He patted Eenie's head indulgently and spoke to the others. "Now dears, I can take you to the borders, but I'm afraid that's as far as I go."

"We're trying to get back to Aequalis," Julian said.

"Oh, you should have said!" The Elder gave a short, garbled laugh. "And how very forgetful of me. The Professor knew you would come across me again eventually. He left me his journal, and I completely forgot to give it for you."

At this the group looked alert.

The Elder withdrew a tattered looking book from his robes.

"I think we've seen that before," said Julian, recognising the cover. "Lee, you found this in the library and showed it to me on my birthday, remember?"

"That's right!" Lee exclaimed. "It mentioned our parents."

The five crowded around it.

"What's it doing here?" Lee asked the Elder.

"The Professor gave it to me for safekeeping when you were all in the dark worlds," he explained. "He was worried, because you were about to go into Libertas, so he left it with me. It's yours now, so look after it."

The Skilled Book suddenly jerked, and Julian almost lost his grip on it. "Hey!" he exclaimed as the book flipped its pages and jerked again.

"What's wrong with it?" Edward said, eyebrows quirking.

"It's trying to get away, I think," Julian held on to it tightly, but the Skilled Book gave one final twist and fell to the floor. Its pages shuffled quickly and opened to a page. Edward immediately knelt down and read the text out loud:

"Inferior books,
Read if you will,
Mediocre knowledge
Same as pigswill."

Edward snorted. "It's jealous!" He laughed with delight.

"It's jealous?" Maggie said.

"Probably because we're reading another book," Julian said with a wry grin.

The Skilled Book flipped its pages again and closed with irritated snap.

"Well, you're not telling us anything useful!" Edward said to it. It tetchily snapped its cover again. The siblings laughed. Edward stood up with the book and passed it to Julian, who gave it a fond pat and put it in his bag.

Lee took the Professor's journal from the Elder and opened it. She skimmed the pages quickly, not finding anything of importance. Getting frustrated, she was about to give up when a thought occurred to her. "Eenie, the microphone!"

Eenie jumped up, eager to help. She took the microphone from her pocket and held it up to her sister. Lee gave her wrist a quick squeeze and directed her to point it at the journal.

"Just hold it up like you did before," Lee said encouragingly.

"I'll do it," said Edward impatiently, snatching the microphone out of Eenie's hand. Her lip quivered but she took a step back.

Edward held the microphone up to the journal. Nothing happened. He shook it in frustration. Eenie went to move forward again but stayed still when Edward frowned at her.

The Elder bellowed, "Boy! Don't be so stupid!"

Edward jumped and turned to face him. "What do you mean?" he sulked.

Lee watched the bald, brown man with the orange cowl stare furiously at the blond-haired boy, defiant in his stare back. *He always hates being called stupid*, Lee thought. She couldn't help but enjoy the dressing down the Elder was giving Edward.

"The microphone is not yours to command! Don't be so arrogant!" The Elder gestured to Eenie. "It will only work for her!"

"Why would it work only for her?" Edward muttered.

The Elder looked disapproving. "Surely you realise by now that her power is amplification? She absorbs and magnifies the rest of your powers. That's how she makes you the five-as-one!"

There was silence as the others took this in.

"Of course!" Julian smacked his hand to his forehead. "Why didn't we realise that?"

They all looked at Eenie, who turned a bit pink under their intense gaze.

"That's why Mediarn kept her as long as he did," the Elder went on, his tone now hushed at the mention of the evil sorcerer. "He was trying to find a way to use her to amplify his own twisted powers."

The mention of Mediarn had a sobering effect on the

group. They were silent as they looked at Eenie, her face turning a deeper pink under the scrutiny.

Julian crouched down next to his little sister. "Eenie, you have an amazing power," he said gently. "To be able to absorb and magnify other powers will be a marvellous skill to develop." Eenie smiled at him tentatively, her blue eyes intense.

Edward had the grace to look shamefaced. "I'm sorry, Eenie. I was being a brat." He held out the microphone. "This is yours."

She took it gratefully, and Edward touched her shoulder lightly in apology.

Eenie looked at the microphone with a small smile, then held it out like a sword at the journal.

"Aequalis!" she announced in a small yet clear voice. The others smiled at her fierce expression. They watched in a moment of silence before they heard the familiar crackling sound. The five grinned at each other as the words slowly drifted out to them.

"Aequalis . . . Aequalis . . . Aequalis . . ."

Eenie handed the journal back to Lee, who looked down at the open page. Skimming the words, she gave a small gasp of excitement.

"Look!" Everyone, including the Elder, crowded around to read the words.

"The Delliks came to see me today while I was camped at Canterbury Fair. Michael brought me my favourite flowers—poppies, roses and lilies."

Lee smiled at this. "I have a really nice memory of Dad putting flowers in my room," she said to the others.

"Me too," Maggie said softly.

They read on.

"The key, which they passed on to me, brought them through from Aequalis. I will need to leave it with someone for safekeeping.

"Who has the key?" Maggie asked.

Lee shrugged and scanned the tiny cramped writing on the page. "There's no more on it." She looked disappointed.

"Not one for being descriptive, was he?" Edward said, flicking his blond fringe out of his eyes.

"You don't have a key from the Professor?" Lee asked the Elder, expecting the answer to be no.

He smiled. "Of course I do." The five stared at him in consternation.

"Well, why haven't you given it to us?" Edward muttered, exasperated.

The Elder gave a short laugh. "You didn't say you wanted a key."

Edward snorted in annoyance.

"There's someone at the foot of the mountains who can guide you from here," the Elder said helpfully. "Come, I will escort you to your miraculous travelling vehicle."

The five giggled at this description of their bathtub. They followed him out of the encampment. Lee glanced at the potted plant as they left and was taken aback—it was now in full bloom.

They followed the Elder to the edge of the encampment, where Julian had hidden the bathtub behind a pile of rocks. Distant chanting floated over to them as they climbed into the tub.

"What's that lovely sound?" Maggie asked.

"It's the mantras," the Elder said, giving her his hand to help her into the tub. "The people here call them hymns. They have meaning and they hold power."

"How?" Maggie asked, intrigued.

"They have harnessed the power of music through their mantras, even though it may seem a primitive form to you," said the Elder, helping Eenie into the tub. "It must be used carefully though."

"Why is that?" Maggie said.

Julian gave a grunt as the bathtub wobbled and started to rise.

"Hold on Julian, I'm still talking," said Maggie, a little crossly.

Julian stayed the bathtub, hovering mid-air but the Elder waved them on. "You go, dears. Go on, travel safely now."

He waved at them, his bright orange robe flapping in the wind. He rapidly turned into a smaller and smaller speck as the bathtub rose from the ground until just a bright orange dot could be seen. The five skimmed over the mountains peaks as they shot off into the distance.

14

The bathtub clipped the side of the mountain with an almighty crash. Lee had been snoozing, and woke with a jolt.

"What's happening?" she cried in alarm.

"JULIAN!" Maggie yelled, shaking him hard. Julian had fallen asleep. He awoke, startled.

"Julian's lost control of the bathtub!" Edward said frantically as the bathtub plummeted.

"Wassshappening?" Julian mumbled deliriously. The group screamed as the ground rushed up at them far too quickly, and their knuckles turned white holding onto the edges of the bathtub. The force of the fall made Lee feel like she'd left her stomach behind and her chest rose and fell as she took in panicked gulps of air.

The wind keened sharply as they plummeted through the air. Their ears became unbearably sore from the sudden drop in altitude.

Eenie grasped Julian's arm, and suddenly the bathtub stopped falling and floated just a few inches off the ground.

"What's happening?" Julian was abruptly alert as he took in the situation.

"YOU FELL ASLEEP!" Edward roared in anger.

"What? Why are we floating? I'm not doing anything," Julian wondered, confused and still groggy with sleep.

The group looked at Eenie holding onto Julian with a firm grip. The bathtub floated down the last few inches until it was steady on the ground. The group shook their heads frantically from side to side, trying to unblock their ears. With a sigh of relief, Lee felt her ears finally pop.

"Did you do that, Eenie?" Maggie asked with an odd look.

Eenie nodded and smiled brightly. "I thought Julian needed help."

"Bloody right he needed help!" Edward snorted and shook his head at Julian.

Julian had gone bright red, now fully awake. Looking back at his siblings, he said guiltily, "I'm so sorry, guys, it won't happen again."

Edward snorted again and jumped out of the bathtub. Julian grasped Eenie's hand and pulled her to him, hugging her. "Thanks for helping, Eenie."

Eenie nodded. "I helped get us to the other places too!"

The four older Delliks looked at each other, surprised. They all smiled broadly at the sudden realisation.

"Eenie!" Maggie cried in happiness.

Julian laughed, shaking his head in bemusement. "No wonder we've been getting everywhere so quickly!"

Lee, Edward and Maggie nodded, awed by their little sister's abilities.

"Explains why we've been protected from the elements

as well," Edward said. "It's like the bubble she created to protect us from the sandstorm."

"How'd you do it, Eenie?" Maggie asked curiously. "Did you take Julian's powers?"

"More like sharing it, I think," Julian said with wry smile. "I don't know what I would have done without you." He gave his little sister another hard hug. Her response was muffled by his jumper. ". . . moved the air . . . "

Lee followed the others out of the tub and took a good look at where they'd landed. Edward had wandered off, massaging his lower back. The mountain peak was directly above them. Snow covered its peak, but brown crags of stone could be seen jutting out here and there.

Lee narrowed her eyes as she looked up at it. "Maggie, can you see that?"

Maggie peered up at the craggy peak.

"Is that . . . ?" Maggie said wonderingly.

"A dragon!" Lee finished her sentence.

"Whoa!" Edward had just spotted it as well, and walked back to join them.

The dragon was pure white, and not immediately noticeable against the snowy peak, which it was wrapped around like a curled-up cat. It had two wings folded in on its back and a long, curling, pronged tail. The dragon's head was covered in sharp spikes, and it rested its snout on the very tip of the mountain.

"It's huge!" Julian exclaimed.

"Is it friendly?" Edward asked Maggie.

She looked a little frightened. "Definitely not." She hunched her shoulders. "I don't think I should have tried to talk to it just now."

The dragon uncurled its long, scaly tail and bellowed into the sky. It turned its massive head towards the five, and they could see flames in its glinting yellow eyes. With another roar, the dragon unfurled its great wings and stretched them out against the sky. The wings were ugly to look at—translucent skin stretched tightly across bony membranes. It bellowed again, this time sounding angrier as it kept its beady eyes on the group.

The five backed away slowly as the dragon clenched its talons and caused rocks and stones to roll down the mountain. It looked like it would spring off the mountainside at any moment. The dragon roared again. Its force had them reeling, and they looked at Julian, starting to panic.

"Quick! Let's get into the bathtub!" They bolted over to it, not needing any further encouragement. Julian helped the girls in and tried to concentrate over the dragon's roars. As the bathtub started to rise slowly from the ground, they clutched the sides in fear.

The dragon gave a furious cry as it watched the bathtub gain momentum, and launched its enormous scaled body off the mountain with deadly force. Its talons clipped the peak of the mountain as it sprung away. The five watched in horror as a sizeable rockslide tumbled down the slope. The ringing sound of rock on rock echoed across the landscape, a tumbling mass of dirt and grit sloughing after them, almost as loud as the dragon's bellows of fury.

The dragon's wings whipped through the air with sinuous movements. Its mouth opened wide and flames shot out. The roar seemed to go on forever.

"Julian, oh my God, HURRY UP!" Edward's knuckles were white as he clasped the edge of the tub.

Julian bowed his head and put his hands to his ears as he tried to concentrate.

"Eenie, can you help him?" Lee urged. Eenie was tucked into a ball in the corner of the tub, looking terrified.

"She's too scared, Lee," Maggie said, terrified herself.

The dragon's scaly form closed in, but the bathtub finally gained some speed and whizzed through the air. The dragon was faster though, and started to gain on them inch by inch. Flames burst out of its scaly mouth again; the group could now hear fire crackling in the frosty air.

"JULIAN!"

The next shot of flames licked the edges of the bathtub.

"GET BACK!" Edward pulled Lee, who had been watching the dragon, back from the edge.

"It's almost got us!" Maggie screamed as the dragon's enormous head drew level with the bathtub.

The dragon opened its mouth, and the group stared down the throat of the enormous beast. Its razor sharp teeth were only inches away. They could see the pit of fire within, and they watched in terror as a ball of flame rolled down its tongue . . .

CRACK!

The dragon twitched, and suddenly its huge body went slack. Its enormous scaly wing clipped the bathtub as the beast plummeted out of the sky.

"ARRRRGGGH!" The group screamed as one.

The bathtub was knocked into the side of the mountain. Julian muttered fiercely as he battled to hold it steady. Rocks and tiny shards of stone flew into their faces as the tub slid dangerously down the slope.

"HOLD ON!" Julian roared as the bathtub slid and slipped down the mountainside. The five held on for dear life. With a final tearing scrape against the rock, the bathtub shattered at the bottom of the slope, and the group tumbled out in different directions.

"Eenie!" Lee crawled to where her little sister was lying limp on the ground. Gently scooping her up, she cradled her in her arms.

"Lee?" Eenie whispered tremulously.

"Oh, thank goodness!" Lee hugged her as Eenie put her arms around her sister's neck.

Maggie sat up unsteadily nearby and shot them a dull-eyed look. She rubbed her head, blinking furiously.

"I'm sorry, I just couldn't hold it steady at the end," Julian said miserably, coming over to them. He walked a little unsteadily. "The force of being knocked out of the air like that was just so strong."

"All good, bro." Edward appeared unscathed, and he clapped his brother on the back. "You did a great job getting us to the ground alive."

Julian tried to smile back, but Lee could see he wasn't happy.

"I turned the rocks we were about to land on into feathers," Edward told them, responding to their questioning looks. Lee shook her head as he grinned widely at them.

"What happened to the dragon?" Maggie asked.

They looked over to where the huge beast had fallen. Standing over the unconscious body was a white, willowy figure with her hands raised over the beast. She looked over at the five and waved merrily.

"It's the white lady!" Edward exclaimed.

"You saved us!" Lee cried, clasping her hands together.

"Thank you so much!" Maggie said fervently. Voices tumbled over each other as they all spoke at once.

"What are you doing here?" Julian queried.

Lee thought he looked a little put out. *Probably because she's saved the day*, she mused.

The white lady smiled benignly and came over to them. "The beast won't hurt you now," she said in her high-pitched voice. "I put him into a deep sleep."

"How'd you do that?" Maggie asked curiously.

"Why, it's my power of course," she said, her dilated pupils looking even bigger than usual.

"You have a power too?" Edward looked surprised.

"Of course!" She laughed trillingly. "You're not the only ones with gifts."

"How do you know we have gifts?" Edward frowned slightly.

"Everyone with gifts knows of the infamous Five." The white lady smiled glowingly at them. "I didn't realise who you were when I first met you," she went on. "How excited I was when I realised!"

Julian muttered something under his breath and changed the subject. "The bathtub's broken. I don't suppose you have any ideas on how we can get down?"

"We're going to have to trek down the rest of the mountain, I'm afraid," she said, smiling brightly. She patted down her tight white trousers and fitted white shirt, which were somehow immaculate despite the rocks and dust around them. Gesturing for the five to follow her, she started hiking down the steep cliff.

The group followed her uncertainly, Julian giving Eenie and Maggie a hand down the rockier parts of the mountain. It was slow going, mainly because they had to wait for the younger ones to catch up. It wasn't long before they were all red in the face and panting hard with exertion. Julian soon realised he could use his powers to move the rocks ahead of them out of the way. It was much easier going after that.

Edward took the lead, shouldering Lee out of the way. She playfully socked him on the arm and muscled her way to the front again. They started to jog a bit, trying to outpace each other.

"Not so fast!" Julian yelled at them as they both ran down the mountain. Edward and Lee looked almost as if they were skiing as they slid down the dirt.

"Careful!" the white lady warned.

Lee almost lost her footing but steadied herself by grabbing Edward.

"ARGH!" Edward flailed and lost his balance, landing on his backside with a hard thump. Lee laughed at his surprised expression. They waited for the others to catch up to them at the bottom of the mountain. There, they all expectantly turned to the white lady.

"This is where I leave you, I'm afraid," she explained.

"But why?" Maggie asked.

"I need to get back," she said with her ever-glowing smile. "I'm glad I was able to be of service to you all again."

"Are you sure you can't come with us?" Edward tried to sound nonchalant, but failed dismally.

"I'm afraid I can't."

Lee, admiring her outfit, noticed a small bump in her tight trouser pocket. *I wonder what that is? she thought. And come to think of it, how on earth did she know we were here, on this very strange and remote mountain?* Lee was about to ask when a bright shimmer appeared around the white lady.

"Goodbye all!" she waved. The shimmer hung in the air as the white lady disappeared into nothingness.

The five exclaimed in astonishment as a large white snowflake appeared in her place. It floated away gently in the wind. They watched it, bemused.

"Wow!" Edward enthused. "Her powers must be strong. I haven't seen anything like that before."

"The Professor disappeared all the time," said Maggie, poking him in the side with her elbow.

"I think it's got more to do with how pretty she is," Julian smirked.

The girls laughed as Edward turned crimson. He went to make a smart retort when a familiar *miaow* sounded nearby.

"Chopsticks!" Maggie cried, kneeling down, her face creasing with happiness. The others rolled their eyes as the errant cat sauntered back into Maggie's eager arms. Chopsticks looked completely unconcerned as she gazed back at them with her one brown and one blue eye.

"Right." Julian said. His smile disappeared as he looked around at their surroundings. "I need to figure out how to get us out of these mountains."

15

The Delliks gazed at the high rocky peaks that surrounded them, muttering amongst themselves. They were starting to feel disheartened when Eenie scrambled to her feet and pulled at Maggie's top. She pointed at a familiar figure with a busy red beard, standing slightly above them on one of the rocky outcrops.

"Mr Lennon!" Maggie exclaimed.

His tall frame held stiff and straight as he watched them scramble over the rocks towards him.

"Interesting way to get down the mountain," he said in his dry voice.

Lee rubbed her legs. "Interesting is one way to put it," she muttered, trying to massage the knots out.

"How did you know to come here?" Julian asked.

"The music," Mr Lennon explained.

"Of course," Edward muttered under his breath.

Mr Lennon swung his dark eyes towards Edward. "It's hard to read at the moment," he growled. "I was lucky to find you at all."

"What do you mean, 'it's hard to read'?" Maggie asked.

After a heavy pause, he told them, "Someone is using the music to convey messages. But not in a good way." He gnawed at his bottom lip, creating a bloodied mark that stood out even against the red mess of his beard. "Words are being used . . ." He trailed off.

"So?" Edward said.

Mr Lennon swung his black glare over to him. "So! You know so little, child."

Edward's face darkened.

Lee quickly said, "We need to get to Aequalis." Her words had the desired effect, and Mr Lennon turned to her, forgetting about Edward and his impudence.

She took the iron key out of her pocket and handed it to him. "We were told this would take us through any one of the gateways." He took it and looked at it, expressionless.

"Yes, it will," he said, handing it back to her. "There's a gateway in the 27 club. I can take you there."

"The 27 club?" Lee queried.

"Yes." Mr Lennon turned his dark eyes to her. "It's obvious that it's an important place, when you think about it."

"What do you mean?" Edward asked.

"Twenty-seven ties back to the magic number of five," said Mr Lennon. "Taking the numbers as stand-alone."

"It equals nine?" Maggie asked, confused.

"Not if you subtract them," said Mr Lennon with the faintest lip twitch.

"How do we get there, sir?" Julian asked politely.

Mr Lennon took a short, silver flute from his inner jacket pocket. He gave them a wry smile. "The most ordinary-looking things are usually the most powerful." He put it to his lips, and five sharp notes burst out of it.

The group blinked and then blinked again. They were no longer surrounded by rocks as far as the eye could see. They were now in a small jazz lounge. A low buzz emitted from around the room, where people were sitting in wall-to-wall, red velvet-lined booths, talking in low voices. None of them paid attention to the sudden appearance of the motley group.

"This seems familiar somehow," Julian murmured.

Intricate brass lamps softly illuminated the room. A small stage sat at its far end, and a microphone was perched on a long stand at the end closest to the audience. Mr Lennon was already walking away and indicated to them to sit in a small booth at the back. "We wait here," he said, looking over his shoulder.

Lee was curious about something. "What did you mean before, about the music?"

Mr Lennon looked at her stonily. Lee was about to change the subject when he suddenly said, "When there is a musical beat, and there are no words, it holds a certain power."

Lee angled her head towards him to hear better over the noise of the lounge. He went on. "You saw the power yourselves. You defeated the Shutterbugs with it. The beat of the drum was their downfall."

The others nodded, now as intrigued as Lee. Scooting their chairs closer to the table, they leaned in to listen.

"Words on their own carry power too," he continued with the same stony expression. "The *intent* and *vibration* behind a word is where the magic lies."

Lee nodded slowly and opened her mouth with more questions. Looking at her, Mr Lennon put up one hand. Lee closed it with a snap.

"When you put music with words . . . well . . . it can cause all sorts of things to happen. If the melody of the music and the vibration of the word are used just so," he went on, holding his index finger and thumb so they were almost touching, "then an entirely different force can be developed and used." Mr Lennon closed his eyes. "Finally, the frequency at which both these elements are used," he said, opening his eyes, "can cause unimaginable things to occur. I think someone knows about this power. Vibrations carried by certain words . . . Intentions . . . *Evil* intentions . . ." There was a heavy pause. "It's an extremely dangerous tool if put in the wrong hands."

The five stared at him in consternation. Mr Lennon's stony countenance softened slightly as he took in their worried expressions. He looked over his shoulder again at the crowded lounge behind him. Turning back to the group, he shook his head in warning. "We will discuss this more another time."

Someone was approaching their table.

Eenie turned around and grabbed Lee's arm with a small squeak. The others followed suit and gaped at the approaching figure.

It was the woman in the short, pretty red dress depicted in the tapestry back at the house. She stood in front of their table, one hand on her hip, magnificent in the dress, with her red hair tumbling down past her hips.

"My microphone!" Eenie gazed up at her, blinking hard, her cheeks flushed. She opened and closed her mouth, too tongue-tied to say much else. The lady flashed a beatific smile at the little girl.

"I didn't notice those before," Edward murmured.

Lee nodded in amazement.

Springing from the woman's shoulder blades was a pair of glorious red, orange and yellow wings. Their feathers cascaded down her back and trailed on the floor. The Delliks couldn't stop staring at them, Julian in particular. The woman waved her hand in front of his eyes, and he blushed furiously. She gave a throaty laugh. With one hand on her hip, she shook back her beautiful mane of hair. "My name is Bellator."

"So you're a faery?" Edward asked.

She laughed loudly and mockingly, and raised her chin. "I'm a fighter!"

Mr Lennon looked impatient. "They need to get to Aequalis," he said to her. "I can't stay long."

She nodded, and he arose from the table, drawing her to one side. They had an urgent conversation, glancing back at the five constantly. Lee watched and thought Mr Lennon looked worried, while Bellator looked plain haughty. A couple of times an odd sort of expression flitted across the faery's face, but it was too quick for Lee to consider what it meant.

Mr Lennon joined their table again. He gave them a warning before he left. "Just be very careful when you hear music with lyrics."

"What do you mean?" Julian asked.

Mr Lennon looked grave. "Like I told you, lyrics hold greater power because of the intent behind the words. Music with lyrics is far more dangerous than a simple melody." He paused, surveying the group. "Until I find out if my instinct is right, and someone else is using its power, steer clear of any music with lyrics."

With those words, he gave the group a small salute and left.

16

The five were unable to take their eyes off the unusual woman standing before them. Lee thought she looked magnificent—fierce and kind, all at once. She couldn't help but stare at her beautiful eyes and lips.

She shook herself. *Get a grip!* "Can you show us how to get to Aequalis?" she asked, attempting to take charge of the situation. The boys were clearly useless, their mouths agape like goldfish. Bellator turned her head towards her, fixing her with piercing eyes that glinted purple in the soft lamplight.

"Well. You should rest for a moment first," Bellator said in a deep, throaty voice. "I'll show you the way to Aequalis tomorrow morning."

"We're kind of in a hurry," Edward stated.

"Time is relative," she said with soft tone of rebuke. "But then you would know that well, wouldn't you?" She narrowed her eyes at Edward. His fist clenched around the watch in his pocket. He glanced quickly at Lee, then away again.

"What are you talking about?" Lee frowned.

Edward snorted. "She's talking rubbish."

Bellator chuckled. "Many people talk rubbish." She

tossed her hair back. "I am not one of them." She held her hand out and smiled kindly at Eenie. "Come, little one. You shall dine with me tonight."

Eenie eagerly took her hand, following her adoringly to another booth. It was grandly dressed with a linen tablecloth, shining gold cutlery, and tall, crystal-stemmed glasses laid out in a circle in the middle. She sat down with Eenie next to her, the small girl still watching her, captivated.

The others trailed behind, unsure if they were meant to join them, but Bellator gracefully flicked her wrist, inviting them to sit. Waiters appeared, seemingly from nowhere, and filled the tall crystal glasses. They all took a sip of the honey-like drink. The five were enraptured by Bellator's every word, and sat half-stunned as they enjoyed one of the fanciest and most exquisite meals they'd ever had.

It was five courses. It began with grapes, small pieces of smoked meat and dew-flavoured melon. The next course was fish, and some of the most delicate flavors they'd ever tasted. The third course was a large pork roast, apple sauce and sultanas scattered around the roasted meat with tasty green vegetables. The fourth course was a lemon meringue pie lighter than air. And finally, a cheese board with varying crispbreads rounded out their decadent meal.

Apart from the delicious food, the night was interesting in other ways. Edward was clearly trying to impress Bellator while also appearing intimidated. It came out in funny ways. He'd compliment her one moment, then insult her the next.

"Faeries are just from children's tales!" Edward announced loudly.

Bellator laughed and threw him a derisive look. "There's a reason they're called 'faery' tales." He went red and mumbled something like "made up".

"History becomes myths." Bellator raised her chin. "Myths then become faery tales. Ever notice something about those tales?" she asked with a contemptuous snort.

Maggie and Lee looked at her, enthralled, forks poised halfway to their mouths.

Julian was too busy staring at her to notice what she was saying.

Without Maggie's attention, Chopsticks had grown bored, and was weaving between their legs beneath the table.

Bellator went on. "The women who didn't have husbands or boyfriends were always witches. They were ugly. They weren't accepted by society." She shook back her beautiful red hair. A red feather floated onto their table. "The women that found their 'Prince Charming'"—she sneered at this—"were always beautiful and apparently lived happily ever after." She raised her eyebrows. "Interesting stories to tell little girls, aren't they."

Eenie had barely touched her food and simply sat there smiling, adoration written all over her face.

Bellator rose from the corner booth in one swift motion. The boys and Lee watched her walk away, her colourful wings shimmering in the light.

Maggie clicked her fingers in front of their faces. "We need to start planning for Aequalis," she said firmly. They blinked and turned to her to listen. "Even though the world is liberated, it might still have traces of Mediarn's influence."

Julian squared his shoulders and nodded. "You're right. Some of his dark magic might have lingered."

Chopsticks leapt up next to Lee and nosed at her pocket with a low purr.

"Eenie is so young to be going back into those worlds," Lee said, concerned.

Edward nodded. "It might bring back bad memories for her, too."

"What do you mean?" Lee asked, nudging the cat away.

Julian nodded at Edward. "If there's anything left of Mediarn, it could do. The Professor told us when she was kidnapped, Eenie was taken through the dark worlds."

Maggie frowned, upset.

"So what should we do?" Lee asked, as Chopsticks nosed the iron key out of her pocket and started playing with it.

The boys shrugged.

"She's taken a real liking to Bellator," Maggie said.

"Maybe Bellator can look after her when we go?" Julian suggested. "We won't be gone long."

"Can she be trusted?" Edward said.

"That's a good idea," said Lee simultaneously.

They looked at each other.

"She'll be safer here than travelling with us," Lee said. She snatched the key from the cat and jammed it back in her pocket.

"Can she be trusted?" Edward said again.

"She's friends with Mr Lennon. He's a friend of the Professor."

"Mmm," Edward grunted.

"You're just saying that because she puts you in your place," Maggie said airily. Edward's blush confirmed her words.

* * *

Minds made up, the four older siblings approached Bellator at breakfast the next morning. Lee handed her the iron key, and she nodded and passed it back. "To get to Aequalis, you just go under the staircase." She pointed to a dark wooden door carved into the side of the stairs.

"Thank you," Julian said. He cleared his throat awkwardly and nodded at his siblings. "We were also wondering if you might help us by looking after Eenie while we're gone?"

Bellator stood with a hand on her hip, evidently thinking intently. She looked at them for a long moment then raised her chin. "I will look after her," she said. "We will meet you back at your house." With that, she spun on her heel and sashayed away, her wings bouncing slightly at the movement. Tiny feathers floated free behind her.

Lee watched an orange downy feather land on Julian's shoulder. He grabbed at it awkwardly, trying to brush it away. Lee hid a smile as it stayed resolutely on his shoulder. His face flushed.

"Now for the hard part," Maggie said softly. Lee's smile faded quickly.

They approached the breakfast table where Eenie was sitting happily playing with her egg and toast.

Sitting down next to her, Edward cleared his throat self-consciously.

"Eenie," he said softly.

She stopped playing and looked up at him trustingly. He looked helplessly at Julian.

Julian nodded at him. "Eenie, we're going to leave you with Bellator for a little while."

Eenie's face fell. "No . . ."

"It won't be for long, darling," Maggie said in a rush, placing her hand on Eenie's.

Eenie snatched her hand back and stared at them with her huge blue eyes. They grew misty. "No!" she cried again. "Please don't leave me behind!"

Lee put her arm around her shoulder. "It really won't be for long, Eenie," she reassured her. "Where we are going could be very dangerous."

Eenie started to cry in earnest and pushed off Lee's arm. "Don't leave me!"

"We wouldn't want you to get hurt, kiddo." Edward tried to hold her hand, but she snatched it away.

"No!"

She gazed beseechingly up at Julian. He gave her a wobbly smile and started explaining how dangerous it would be, how it wouldn't be for very long, and how the lovely lady with the beautiful wings would be looking after her. "Wouldn't that be nice?" he finished.

Eenie grew stiller as Julian talked. She looked around at all their faces. Maggie shifted from foot to foot. Edward tried to grin at her, but failed. Lee watched her, eyes welling, mirroring her little sister's. Julian cleared his throat in the silence.

Eenie stared down at the table. "Okay," she said softly. Large tears plopped onto the white tablecloth, leaving wet spots. Lee sensed she wanted to get away—away from her hurt feelings at being left behind.

Bellator suddenly appeared before them. "Come with me, little one," she said in the softest voice, stretching her hand out to the little girl. Eenie gulped and took it. She held herself stiffly upright as her siblings each gave her a hug and said goodbye. She didn't meet their eyes.

Bellator, still holding Eenie's hand, waved at them as they left. Lee looked back at the stunning redhead holding the hand of the tiny blond girl, whose small shoulders shook as she choked back sobs.

With a heavy heart, Lee followed her siblings.

17

Taking the key out of her pocket, Lee fitted it into the old-fashioned lock and turned it twice, clockwise. The door swung open, revealing the gloom beneath the staircase. With a deep breath, she stepped through.

Maggie followed, holding Chopsticks. With a shrill miaow, the cat bounded gracefully out of her arms in one long leap, and bolted back through the door just as it slammed shut behind them.

"Chopstiiiicks!" Maggie wailed, her empty arms still bent in a cradling position.

"She'll be fine," Julian said, rubbing her arm briskly.

The others spoke to comfort her, but not very enthusiastically, largely glad they were again free of the annoying creature.

Standing in the next world, Lee looked around curiously. Heavy jungle foliage surrounded them—the source of the gloom. Thick, outstretched branches blocked out most of the sunlight. Tiny arrows of light struggled through the dense, leafy canopy, now and then bursting brightly onto the dark muddy floor to create strange, dappled patterns on the ground.

Bizarre sounds surrounded them, those of exotic birds

and small animals calling to each other in low throbbing chirrups and high-pitched warbles.

"The door's disappearing!" Maggie noted quietly. The others watched as it slowly faded. With a shimmer it disappeared entirely. "Hey guys . . ." Maggie continued, trailing off uncertainly.

"What?" Edward asked.

"I don't really remember Aequalis being like this." Maggie stared at their surroundings wide-eyed. The others gazed up at the huge and imposing redwood trees towering over them like bark-covered giants.

"There wasn't a jungle last time," Edward frowned.

"We were floating last time too," said Lee, looking at her feet planted firmly on the muddy ground.

"Where's the sinking city?" Maggie wondered, turning in a semi-circle as she looked around her.

Edward's forehead wrinkled. He stared up at the trees. "I think we might be in Consecutio," he said slowly. "In fact, I'm sure of it." He glowered at the trees and ducked his head.

"Don't use your powers here," Julian said in an undertone to his brother, who nodded gravely, unusually silent in his agreement.

"How did we get to Consecutio?" Lee said. "The Professor's journal said the key was the gateway to Aequalis."

"Maybe the Elder gave us the wrong one," Maggie sighed.

Lee took the key out of her pocket and examined it

closely. She felt a cold shiver travel up her spine.

"The key's changed," she said quietly.

"What do you mean, the key's changed?" Maggie said.

"I mean, it's a different key!" Lee's voice was sharp.

"How can that be?" Edward snatched it from her and examined it. He grew quiet. "You're right. It had two edges when the Elder gave it to us." He traced the bottom of the key with his finger, before handing it to Julian.

"Now it has three," said Julian, turning it deftly in his fingers. The four were silent as they stared at the key.

"At least we're back in the dark worlds," Julian said finally. "The worlds are linked, so I'm sure we can find our way to Aequalis from here."

They glanced around uneasily. They were dwarfed by the sequoias' long branches stretching out like giant green umbrellas, concealing them from most of the sunlight. The jungle around them was incredibly dense, and it felt as if they were enveloped in its shadowy gloom.

"I feel like an ant," Maggie observed, as she stared up at the strong, silent giants.

"The trunks are almost as wide as the farmhouse!" Lee exclaimed. As she stood gaping at the goliaths, she noticed something. "Look, stairs!"

Sure enough, a set of rickety wooden stairs led up into the trees. The four craned their necks. A small wooden platform sat high above their heads. Long ropes and wooden planks formed a suspension bridge that led to another platform on the next tree.

"I wonder who built those?" Maggie pondered, rubbing her neck.

"There was the tribe here before," Lee remembered.

Edward looked at Julian questioningly.

"I can hold the bridges steady if they start to fall apart," Julian said reluctantly.

With a whoop, Edward bolted to the stairs and started climbing them.

"We need to find another door," Julian said to the girls. "That's as good a place as any to start looking." He stared up at the swaying bridges in resignation.

Lee was close behind Edward on the rickety stairs. They creaked under her feet as she bounded up them, as eager as Edward to walk amongst the treetops.

Reaching the top, the four stood crowded together on the small wooden platform, which swayed lightly in the breeze. They surveyed the treetops, linked together in the dense and tightly-knit canopy like a green and brown rippling ocean. A long way below them, the dirt ground was a distant spatter of muddy brown.

Gingerly testing the swaying bridge with her foot, Lee braved it to go first. The others followed slowly in silence, walking single file along the narrow bridge amongst the treetops. The ancient wooden planks creaked ominously, and the ropes groaned as the weight of the group scraped the swaying, quivering bridge against the tree trunks.

They soon realised the bridges formed a large loop around the treetops, circling back to where they'd started.

It did, however, afford them a magnificent view of where they were and what surrounded them.

"What's that?" Maggie asked, drawing their eyes to the distant south, where, through the trees, they could see puffs of smoke slowly escaping a huge vent in the earth.

"I think it's a volcano," said Edward. He looked at it with interest. "We should head towards it. It seems like the only thing around here that might have a doorway near to it or through it."

Julian shrugged. "It's as good a plan as any. Let's camp here for the night and start afresh tomorrow."

18

After climbing back down from the treetop bridges, the four walked for a few minutes until they found a spot that was less densely forested. Edward conjured up another sock tent, and they quickly and efficiently went about getting things ready to eat and sleep.

Edward suggested they start a fire, but Julian shut down the suggestion immediately.

"Remember, actions have strong consequences here," Julian said, directing a dark frown at his brother.

"I know!" Edward muttered, throwing his backpack onto his makeshift bed, harder than necessary. "I'm not stupid twice."

Lee wondered what they meant, but figured Julian was just warning him against his usual pranks. They had enough food from Bellator to last them a while, although it wasn't anything fancy, and they chomped happily on nuts, dates, fruit, dried meats and bread.

* * *

They slept fitfully that night, and the next day were up and packed quickly. They spent all morning walking towards the distant crater. It was slow going as there was no straight path, and they kept having to weave in and out of the densely packed trees.

Edward led the way with the girls in the middle and Julian at the back. The tree branches hung over them like brown, beckoning fingers, trails of bark hanging off them in tendrils.

"I hope we find the Professor soon," Julian muttered, almost to himself. Lee overheard and slowed her walk to match his, so that they were side by side. Sensing the responsibility was starting to overwhelm him, she clasped his arm.

"The Box will surely be the last piece of the puzzle," she said softly. Lee had wrapped it in her jumper and packed it safely next to the Skilled Book in her backpack.

Julian shrugged but said nothing.

They walked for a couple of hours, the earth beneath their feet becoming ever muddier as the day wore on. Their legs throbbed from walking on the sloppy and uneven surface. They became irritable, Edward being the most vocal on how tough going it was.

"My calves are sore," Edward whined, stopping abruptly to rub them. The muddy water on the ground rippled as the wind picked up overhead.

Lee stared at the forest floor, concentrating on putting one foot before the other, blocking out Edward's complaining. She blinked. The muddy floor seemed to pulsate slightly. She shook her head, thinking her eyes were playing tricks.

"My ankles ache!" cried Edward, stopping again. The others walked around him as he stood there grumbling. Lee was last and noticed the mud seemed to swell around Edward's feet more than anywhere else.

"This jungle is so DARK!" Edward threw his hands in the air and stomped after the others. The mud beneath him rippled again, forming whorls and patterns in the sludge.

Lee was still staring at the ground and could have sworn the mud was converging to form an indistinct shape. Julian seemed to be in one of his silences again and was tuning out Edward, walking on with his head down and shoulders hunched.

"The volcano must be miles away!" Edward whined again, squelching towards the girls. Maggie and Lee rolled their eyes at each other. "How much longer is there to go?"

"Edward, shut UP!" Maggie finally yelled.

Lee looked back at her brother and squinted, not entirely sure of what she was seeing. The rippling mud looked like it was progressively creeping towards him.

"Yuck! What is this?" Maggie lifted her foot. The soggy, sludgy mud hung off her shoe in slimy tendrils.

"What's THAT?" Lee yelped, pointing behind Edward. They all turned to see the slinky trails of mud form a strange and distinct shape. With a horrible sticky sound, the mud formation grew slowly and steadily bigger as it rose from the forest floor.

The four gaped as the mud piled up in a heap and started to slowly squelch towards them. The form looked almost humanoid as it advanced on the group, lurching and stumbling, long trails of mud and dirt dangling off it in an eerie resemblance of limbs.

"What . . . what is it?" Maggie cried, her voice shaking.

"I don't know, but I don't think we should stick around to find out," stated Edward. He looked at his brother expectantly.

Julian was about to use his powers to blow the mud monster apart, then had second thoughts, remembering where he was.

There were four yells as they all thought the same thing at once. "RUN!"

They bolted from the mud monster as fast as they possibly could, Edward throwing sticks at it over his shoulder, which clattered uselessly to the ground as they slid down the muddy creature.

Luckily, the monster didn't seem very well-equipped to chase them as clods of mud and dirt fell off it, creating holes throughout its body. Its strange legs eventually gave way, and it fell to the ground with a sickening squelch. The four ran furiously, keen to get as much distance between it and them as possible. Eventually they collapsed in a heap under a tree, chests heaving, as they tried to catch their breath.

"What WAS that?" Maggie exclaimed, panting.

"This place is strange," sighed Julian, a crease appearing between his brows. "The quicker we find that door the better." Murmuring their agreement, they took a break to eat something and rest. In single file, they walked for the rest of the day, using the craggy volcano as their compass.

19

The third day was much the same. The Delliks ate break-fast with sparse conversation, the unspoken intent to find the next doorway prominent in all their thoughts. Lee thought their new path was more monotonous. Every tree looked the same, and the hard-packed earth formed a seemingly unending path.

As they passed through the tightly-packed tree trunks, they noticed a faint buzzing overhead. Swarms of insects were clustered around the treetops. They seemed to glow with a fluorescent spark. A couple of lone insects left the larger swarm and floated towards them.

"They're like fireflies," Lee murmured, watching as the insects clustered together, lighting up the tree up like Christmas lights.

"They're wasps," Maggie proclaimed. She chuckled dryly at the change in Lee's expression. The others laughed as Lee shrank back from the tiny bug, buzzing too close for her comfort. They watched the swarm fly from one tree to another like a giant glowing ball, buzzing harmoniously.

As they walked on, the trees surrounding them became even denser, the murky gloom deepening to heavy shadows. Tempers became shorter as their legs ached, and their bite-sized comments to one another grew progressively shorter and snappier as the day wore on.

"Chopsticks has probably forgotten all about you," Edward said to Maggie, his lip curling nastily. The wasps overhead droned incessantly.

Maggie's face darkened. "Shut it," she muttered. She looked like she wanted to say more, but settled for a withering stare and stalked off. The swarm of wasps became increasingly shrill.

Edward wouldn't leave it alone. "It was just a cat," he sneered. "Get over it." He kicked up some dirt in front of him that splattered across the back of Maggie's legs.

Maggie stopped dead, and turned around to face him, her violet eyes dark. "Leave it!"

The drone of the wasps seemed to get louder. As Maggie and Edward bickered, Lee watched the wasp swarm pulsate slightly, then suddenly double in size.

"She only wanted you for food," Edward sniped.

Maggie's eyes flashed as she muttered something cutting in reply.

"Why do you want a cat anyway? They just get in the way."

Maggie clenched her hands by her sides, her eyes darkening. The wasps swelled, and their buzzing turned ominous.

"Her eyes were gross too. They didn't match," said Edward. The droning deepened with an ugly undertone. Maggie looked furious, a disconcerting expression on her usually kind face. The buzzing became deafening as Maggie turned a deep purple, fighting to keep her temper. Her eyes were now a colour they'd only seen once before.

Lee yelled at Edward to stop, not exactly sure why, but certain it was important they calm Maggie down.

The wasps were ear-splitting as they swarmed in earnest, heading directly towards the group.

Lee gasped and grabbed Julian's arm. The tree trunks looked as if they were moving. Lee realised in horror that snakes and spiders slithered and crawled along them at an alarming rate.

Edward realised his mistake too late. "Maggie, I'm sorry, I didn't mean it."

The huge swarm of wasps enveloped Maggie. She yelled something to the others, but her words were lost in the deafening drone. Julian and Edward picked up nearby sticks and raised their arms, ready to beat the wasps away. Suddenly the wasp colony soared off into the sky, a huge, angry, glowing ball, the buzzing fading as they flew away.

They rushed to Maggie, who shook all over. Her arms were covered in huge, angry red welts.

"I've been stung," she said in a strangled voice. Her face turned white, and she dropped to her knees. "I feel really dizzy."

They crowded round her, feeling helpless, thoughts racing.

"What do we do, what do we do?" cried Lee, wringing her hands. Maggie was now on her hands and knees in the mud. Her breathing grew more laboured.

"Do something!" Edward yelled at Julian. Julian crouched down next to his sister, his face white and tight. He gently held Maggie's swollen arms.

Edward and Lee fell silent as they watched him close his eyes, muttering quietly. With a concentrated effort, he used his powers to draw the poison from Maggie's arms.

Lee and Edward's concern gradually turned to awe as they watched their brother work. Slowly, the glutinous, toxic venom leeched out of Maggie's arm, trickling harmlessly to the ground.

After a few moments, Julian sat back on his heels with a small sigh. Maggie groaned and got to her knees. Unsteadily, she rose to her feet to the relieved murmurs of her brothers and sister.

"God, I'm sorry Maggie," Edward sounded wretched. His hair was sticking up all over the place where he'd been pulling at it. "I don't know what happened," he said, taking one of her hands. "I never thought an animal would attack you!"

Maggie clenched her hand in his and smiled wanly. "Me neither."

"It all happened so quickly," said Lee.

Maggie nodded. "I was too angry at Edward to even notice what was happening."

"Why did they attack you?" Lee wondered.

"I don't know," Maggie replied miserably.

"Did you speak with them?" Julian asked.

Maggie rubbed her arms, which were fading but still showed red welts. "The only time I could speak to them was at the end, but only after they'd stung me. They flew away when I told them to."

They were a subdued bunch after such a shock and decided to camp where they were for the night and start again in the morning. Nightfall seemed to come quickly, the darkness creeping in through the trees as they quietly ate then went to bed.

20

O n the fourth day, they finally felt they were making headway, with the volcano appearing not so far away. Surrounding them on all sides as they walked were heavily darkened trunks. Over their heads were brown-spotted leaves and branches that shivered occasionally in the breeze. Lee thought the day seemed particularly oppressive. The tree giants seemed to close in on them even more, and the gloom and muggy heat became stifling as the day went on. The jungle, already frightening, had taken on an even more sinister feel. Lee swore she could see dark shadows amongst the trees, but dismissed it as part of the dull repetition. "Can we break for lunch soon?" she asked Julian.

He wasn't paying attention, deep in one of his introverted silences, walking ahead of the group, shoulders hunched. The clouds overhead raced across the sky, turning darker with each passing second. The shadows in the trees lengthened, and a lone bat flew out from the branches over their heads.

"He's in one of his moods," Edward whispered to Lee, before suddenly shrieking, "EW!" He pulled a leech off his calf.

Lee wrinkled her nose in disgust. Maggie quickly took the leech from her brother and placed it gently on a nearby tree. Julian barely glanced over, and hunched further down, hands in his pockets.

Lee kept a close watch on her oldest brother, uneasy but unsure why. She tried to draw him out by asking him about lunch again but got a monosyllabic reply. Staring upwards, Lee noticed the small patch of clouds visible through the canopy were almost black, cutting out any sunlight and blanketing them in a dim, grey light.

Julian abruptly stopped, causing Edward to barrel into him. "We can have a break here." He was quiet throughout their small meal and started walking again straight after, barely glancing at the others.

Lee exchanged a look with Edward and Maggie, concern written across each of their faces.

Julian's tense mood and the jungle noises kept them all on edge that afternoon. The previous day's events made them feel as if they were walking on eggshells. Julian seemed to go deeper into his dark mood as they walked on.

Lee felt a shiver travel up her spine, despite the mugginess of the day. Shadows and strange, murky shapes still seemed to quiver amongst the trees. She watched as a couple of bats flew out of the darkened trees. The clouds overhead grew swollen with rain, black and fit to burst.

Maggie tried to talk to Julian about something inconsequential, but he paid her no attention. Edward, too, tried to draw his brother out by teasing him, but got no response.

Trying a new tactic, Lee said to Julian, "You know, you really shouldn't feel guilty about the Professor. It wasn't your fault."

This was a mistake.

"Leave me alone!" Julian yelled, his voice breaking, shocking them all with his ferocity. "You don't know how it feels!" The clouds overhead deepened in colour until they were almost black. Shadows darted here and there amongst the trees. "How worthless I feel, how useless I felt when I couldn't help him." His face tightened with emotion. The clouds rumbled with distant thunder. Julian's voice was tense as he snapped, "It feels like I'm drowning when everyone else around me is breathing!" He swallowed hard and looked away from them, avoiding their eyes. "I felt completely useless when I saw the Professor's body just lying there. What good am I? I'm no use to anyone".

The rumbling on the horizon sounded closer. Sharp daggers of lightning sliced through the air like quicksilver darts, disappearing as quickly as they'd appeared.

Staring unseeingly, Julian said, "I feel completely alone. It's like I'm in a locked room with no light, or windows, or door. It's so dark I can't see my hands in front of my face."

The rumbling deepened, until it sounded like it was right upon them. A thunderous *CRACK* made them all jump.

The four gaped as they watched thunder and lightning take over the sky like a giant game, one player throwing out ferocious darts of light and fire, the other responding with thunderous cracks of sound. Rain lashed their faces and bodies like spitting wet ants.

The land around them, once dark and gloomy, was now alight with lightning, the sky a white-hot electrical maelstrom.

Julian's attention was taken by the stormy sky, and his next words died on his lips. Lee laid a comforting hand on his arm. It seemed to bring him back to himself. He relaxed slightly and smiled somewhat awkwardly at his sister.

"We're here for you," Maggie said quietly.

"We always will be." Edward's blue eyes were unusually serious.

An eerie calm descended as the thunder and lightning disappeared as quickly as it had come. The rain went with it, leaving the group and their surroundings completely drenched.

"We haven't had much luck here, have we?" Julian sighed. The wet, muddy plains would be even harder to traverse than before.

"It's the land of consequence," Maggie said, exasperated, pulling her foot out of the mud with a squelch.

The words triggered something in Lee. "Connected . . . consequence . . . consciousness," she said softly. Her siblings looked at her questioningly. "A vision! Mr Lennon said words are important."

"That's right," said Julian. "He said words carry vibrations."

"I think our words and the emotions behind them are having a strange effect in this place," Lee mused. "They seem to manifest in physical ways."

"What do you mean?"

"Well, think about it. Edward was complaining, and the mud monster appeared."

Julian nodded. "Maggie got mad, and the wasps attacked."

Maggie rubbed her arm self-consciously.

"I've never been unable to tell an animal not to attack me, either," she said, disconcerted at the memory.

"The black clouds and storm rolled in when Julian . . ." Edward trailed off as he looked at his brother.

"I have been pretty stormy lately," Julian said with a reluctant half-smile. He gave a short laugh, and their expressions changed to relief.

They all slept well that night, spirits more buoyed now they better understood the world they were in.

* * *

On the fifth day, mid-morning, they made it to the volcano.

"Finally," Edward mumbled. "I'm sick and tired of this world." He slapped at his skin, squashing a mosquito on his arm.

"It's not the nicest place to get trapped in," Julian said drily.

As they approached they fell silent, awed by the enormous mountainous crater. It sat stoutly, small puffs of smoke escaping from the lip and disappearing into the humid air around it.

"What are we looking for exactly?" Lee asked with a touch of trepidation, staring at the rocky basalt towering before them.

"Anything we can walk through," Julian noted. "We may as well start climbing it." Small groans greeted this suggestion, but they were soon labouring up the slope towards the crater rim. Their feet slipped in the black gravel as they walked, setting them back one step for every two steps forward.

"Wait." Maggie stopped suddenly. "I can hear an eagle nearby who's near a doorway!"

They responded to her words with small cheers, more excited than they'd been in days. They trekked a bit further, following Maggie's eagle, until they approached a strange carved outline in the side of the volcano. They would have walked straight past it if not for the keen eyes of the hunting bird and Maggie keeping an ear out.

Carved within the outline was a keyhole. It was one of the most welcome sights they'd ever seen.

"Get the key, get the key!" Edward exclaimed in relief.

Lee took the key out with quivering fingers and put it into the outlined lock. It sunk into the side of the volcano as if she was pushing into dirt. The outline glowed, and the Delliks cheered again as a golden door appeared and swung open. Jostling each other in their haste, they walked one by one through the glowing entrance.

21

Safely on the other side, the group breathed one huge collective sigh as they watched a cow, munching contentedly, float by.

"We're in Aequalis!" Lee exclaimed as the door shimmered and disappeared behind them. At the others' insistent urging, she pulled the small wooden box carefully out of her backpack. With trembling fingers she opened the lid.

... POP ...

The four knew the sound all too well.

"It's the PROFESSOR!" they shouted in unison.

"That's his sound!"

"He's here!"

"Where is he!?"

The group turned this way and that, trying to see where the Professor was.

"CHILDREN!"

His familiar voice poured over them like honey. There he was, suddenly standing before them, looking smaller and thinner than they remembered, but there he was.

The next few minutes were a frenzy of hugging and shouting.

"We found you!"

"We've looked everywhere for you!"

"How did you survive the fight!?"

The Professor laughed and beamed at them as they grabbed him one by one in a giant bear hug.

After a time, he gestured for them to quieten down so he could speak. Maggie stayed clutching his arm, looking up at him with brimming eyes.

"There's a lot to explain, children, and there will be time enough for all that," he said in his wonderful, rusty voice. "Suffice to say, the Box has been a good friend to me over the years." He looked fondly at the little wooden box. "A story for another time perhaps, but it serves well in moments of desperation, and my power fortunately allows me to transport to all manner of places." He smiled around at them all. "Thank heavens you were able to get it back, Lee."

"We saw Mediarn strike you with the sword!" Julian exclaimed.

"Yes." The Professor was grave for a moment. "Julian, you tried to move the sword away." Julian nodded, and the familiar worry line reappeared between his brows. His face was drawn as he stared at the Professor, waiting tensely to see what he would say next.

"There must have been a tiny skerrick of the five-as-one power that stayed on the sword," said the Professor. He gave Julian a look that was full of pride. "When the sword went through me, it carried that power with it." The

Professor closed his eyes briefly at the memory. "It was enough to transport me to the Box, at any rate. From there I was easily healed."

Lee felt the sheer relief rolling off Julian. His drooping shoulders straightened, his chest rose and fell with relief, and he looked like her big brother again.

"Where's Enid?" the Professor asked, looking around at them.

"We left her with Bellator," said Julian anxiously, waiting for his reaction. "We thought it wouldn't be safe to bring her into the other worlds." He paused. "Not so soon after Mediarn was vanquished."

The Professor nodded, much to their relief. "A sensible decision. There may have been lingering effects, and I haven't been through them since to see if they're completely safe yet."

"We thought as Bellator was a friend of yours . . ." Edward left the sentence hanging.

The Professor laughed heartily and smiled at Edward. "There is no safer person than Bellator to have on your side."

Edward grinned and flushed a little at her name.

The group spoke over each other, asking the Professor question upon question. They talked long into the night, sitting around a campfire Edward had conjured until the sun broke over the horizon.

They told the Professor about all the people they'd met on their travels.

"I was surprised at how helpful everyone was!" Lee remarked.

"If there's one thing travelling has shown me, it's that we are all the same deep down," said the Professor. "This idea of 'us' versus 'them' should not exist." He grabbed a bread roll from the bowl and hungrily ripped off a large corner. "People are inherently good, and people at heart mostly want to help and assist if they can. Mediarn used his power to spawn fear and create conflict, spreading lies that made us think we live in an intolerant, biased, hate-filled world."

"Just as well we vanquished him," Lee said darkly.

The Professor nodded. "Indeed. Travelling like I have, has shown me that we do not live in that kind of world—far from it. It taught me about the world in a way that nothing I read, watched or heard from other people could ever do." He took another bite of bread. "I'm pleased you travelled. Maybe earlier than I would have liked, and under different circumstances, but I will always advise anyone, young or old, to travel." He swallowed and continued. "Indeed. Get out there and see cultures for yourself, and never believe everything you're told."

The four of them nodded in agreement. Passing around dishes of food, they busied themselves with third and fourth helpings and chatted gaily.

"How did you get to Aequalis?" the Professor asked through another large mouthful of bread. "Through Partior again?"

"No, through Consecutio," Lee said.

The Professor almost choked on his food. It took a few moments of hard coughing before he could speak again.

"Consecutio?" he cried, profoundly shocked. They nodded.

Lee felt an icy finger trace up her spine.

"It's so dangerous there," the Professor said, shaking his head, still clearly stunned.

"I got swarmed by wasps there," Maggie shivered. "And I got stung!" She rubbed the faded bite marks on her arm.

"You did?" The Professor rubbed his chin. He looked at the faded bites on Maggie's arm, his eyebrows raised. "Venom . . ." he mused. "Was anyone angry? It *is* the world of consequence." He looked at Maggie intently, taking in her now beet-red expression. "Well." The Professor cleared his throat, his face grave. "Anger is one of the worst emotions you can have in Consecutio. It brings out venomous creatures."

"There were snakes and spiders running along the trees too," Lee reminded the others, shuddering at the memory.

The Professor nodded. "Anger and resentment turn toxic and will eventually poison you," he said to them. Maggie blinked hard and rubbed her arm again. "People can get very sick holding onto anger. You're lucky you weren't seriously hurt."

"We also thought other emotions might have been affecting things around us," Lee suggested.

The Professor nodded. "Yes, you'd be right, Lee. Vibrations carried by certain words, and the intentions behind them, cause physical changes." He looked at them one by one. "In Consecutio, it's all about action and reaction."

The group grimaced at each other, each realising they'd had a lucky escape.

"It's so very dangerous for you to have gone there." He frowned. "You should never have been there without me."

Lee was about to mention the key when the Professor said, "Everything is accelerated there. I told you this, remember? I didn't keep you there for long."

The four nodded.

The Professor went on. "That's because *everything* is accelerated there."

He looked at their confused expressions.

"Everything, including time," he said. "An hour in Consecutio is a month everywhere else."

There was a deathly silence.

"Wait . . . what?" Maggie whispered.

"A MONTH!" Edward exclaimed.

"Oh my God!" Julian cried in a strangled voice.

"EENIE!" they all yelled at once.

"How long were we there for? HOW LONG WERE WE THERE?" Lee had never heard Julian sound so frightened before.

Lee did the sums first, her white face turning even paler.

"Five days . . . " Lee's voice trailed off in horror.

"How much time has passed in our world?" Edward gasped.

Maggie started crying. "Ten years . . ."

"Can't we just go back in time?" Edward cried, anguished, pulling the watch from his pocket.

The Professor's eyes darted back and forth between them. His face had turned whiter with each passing word. He looked distraught. "No." He put his head in his hands. "The watch only works in Consecutio. The outside world remains the same. The power of the watch was bound to that world only, many, many years ago."

"So ten years have passed in the other worlds, too?" Lee asked, closing her eyes.

The Professor nodded, looking haggard and tired.

"I had no idea you had stayed there longer than a few hours," he said. "That is strictly forbidden."

The four of them stared at the Professor, their emotions in turmoil. The implications of what had just happened were overwhelming. Every word of response trailed off in horror, and they each sat blinking, as though in a daze.

The Professor looked as if he'd aged twenty years at once. He slowly rose to his feet. "It's time for us to go home," he said quietly.

They nodded and silently arose to follow him back to the house.

* * *

It had been ten years since she'd last seen her siblings. Enid looked at their picture sitting before her on the dressing table, then at her long blond hair in the mirror. She picked up the scissors. Taking a shiny, golden piece of hair in her hand, she placed the scissor blades around it. With a decisive movement, she closed them with a snap.

She looked at the chunk of blond hair in her hand. It seemed somehow different.

Grinning, she grabbed chunks and snipped them off in precise motions. Several moments later, she looked at her reflection with a raised eyebrow. Her hair was short, choppy and uneven.

She smiled to herself in the mirror and left the room.